SHANTI'S STORY

FOR MY GRANDCHILDREN:

GEORGE, FLORENCE, NINA,

BETHAN, NELLIE AND MATTHEW

Shanti's Story

SLUM KIDS OF CALCUTTA

Maureen Roberts

YOUCAXTON PUBLICATIONS

OXFORD & SHREWSBURY

ISBN 978-1-912419-04-3
Printed and bound in Great Britain.
Published by YouCaxton Publications 2017

YouCaxton Publications
enquiries@youcaxton.co.uk

Contents

A Letter from Shanti

Dear Reader,

My name is Shanti, a name my blessed grandmother gave me. I am fifteen and I live in India. Through some divine plan I was born with deformed legs, which means I have never been able to walk. My life, however, has been one of untold riches. It is a tapestry of happiness and sadness interwoven with the amazing kindness of people.

I met Hamid when we were both lonely and forsaken. He is blind and we make music together. It was our good luck to meet Rupa and become part of a family. Her young sister, dearest Amrita, joined us in our street performances.

This is a story of my life so far: a journey I want to share with you, even though it is not yet complete. I want you to take the memory of me with you. We are all part of one another's journey and will meet together some day.

And one more thing: a secret I will share with you. I will walk one day. First I will stand, then, who knows? Life is a mixture of determination and destiny. For once, for me, fate will do as I say.

Love and best wishes,
Shanti

1

I Will Stand!

Well, that's settled then! The operation will take place next week and he will eventually be able to stand?"

"Yes, eventually. I'm not sure that he will ever walk, but yes, I'm optimistic about the outcome. I've performed similar operations before. They are complicated but usually successful. There is the problem that he is fifteen and not younger. But, as I said, I have performed the operation and I am confident that it will be okay."

In a hospital in India two men were finishing their meeting. They pushed their chairs back, stood up, shook hands and moved out of the room, into a corridor.

"Good! I'll tell him the news, doctor. He's one of our best musical students. I hope he is making the correct decision. He is determined to be able to stand."

The two men shook hands again. The doctor went back into his office, where he sat down in his chair and picked up the X-ray pictures that covered his desk. He looked intently at them, then hung them on a hook on the wall. The X-ray pictures showed leg bones that were twisted and malformed. The doctor paused, then picked up the telephone.

The other man pushed his way through swing doors at the end of the corridor and stepped into the hospital's reception area. He gave the doorman a coin, walked out into the street and hailed a taxi. One stopped almost immediately, he got in and the taxi sped off down the road.

A week later a young man with a mop of unruly hair was wheeled on a trolley down the same corridor. He was taken into a small room adjacent to the hospital's operating theatre. A nurse was waiting for him. She pushed his sleeve back and prepared to give him an injection. Smiling at him, she asked,

"Are you feeling relaxed?"

The young man frowned at her, then uncertainly gave her a small grin.

"Would you be?"

She gently rubbed the spot where the needle had penetrated and asked, as his eyes began to close,

"And what's your name?"

"Shanti, it's Shanti. I remember ..."

"Shush, shush, Shanti."

The nurse stroked his forehead gently.

"Wake up Shanti." The same stroking of his hair and the same gentle voice. Shanti forced himself to open his heavy eyelids. He looked down at the cage of white bedsheets covering his legs. The nurse followed his look and smiled reassuringly at him.

"That's to keep the pressure of the sheets from hurting you."

"How did it go?"

"Well, I think. The doctor seemed very pleased. He'll be round later and will answer all your questions. Do you want a drink?"

Shanti nodded and sipped from the glass of water the nurse held for him. Unable to sit upright, he sank back onto his pillow and he slept.

More weeks of massage, physiotherapy and gentle exercise followed.

The first time Shanti was lifted upright onto his legs, he stared down at them in horror and disbelief. How could they belong to him? They looked skeletal and almost alien. Huge long scars puckered up the thin slack skin. Purplish blotches patterned them in a crazy design. He felt strange pinpricks and flashes of pain. Dizziness overcame him and he hung onto the two nurses supporting him.

"I'll never stand on my own," he blurted out despairingly.

"Yes, you will. It takes time, Shanti." The nurses hugged him close and Shanti leaned against them for a moment. Then, mustering all his strength, he forced himself to stand upright, still hanging onto the nurses. He wobbled, but controlled his balance and let go of the nurses' arms. Everyone cheered as he balanced on his own for a few seconds. He raised his arms in the air and gave a loud 'whoop'. The two nurses caught him as he fell backwards.

"I did it!" he yelled. "I stood on my own!"

That night he slept and remembered once again.

2

The Snake Charmer

Shanti! Shanti! Catch us, spider man!"
The chant resounded around some wooden huts where a group of scruffy children were poking sticks at a little boy with an unruly mop of hair. His legs were terribly deformed and he scurried like a crab along the bare earth. He frantically tried to grab at the sticks and tug his tormentors over, but was overcome by the strength and superior numbers of the opposition. When he was covered in dust and wailing, the group eventually stopped their game. They sat on the ground beside him and pushed him backwards and forwards.

"Shanti! Shanti! Spider man!"

"Shanti! Shanti! Bent legs!"

They only stopped their chanting when a monkey ran across the yard and they all chased after it. Shanti was left wiping his nose on the back of his hand and pulling himself to his hut.

"Crying again!" said his father, when he saw the state of his son. "We'll have to toughen you up. Now you are nearly seven you can help in the fields."

"Can I, dada? Can I really help?"

Shanti looked up hopefully with his big brown eyes at the angry face of his father.

"What can I do?" he continued brightly. "Perhaps I can ride on the water buffaloes when you are planting the paddy fields, dada?"

"Yes! And perhaps you can plant the rice as well." Father scowled at his son. "Listen, Shanti. You are a cripple. You cannot walk, you cannot ride, you cannot help! The only thing you can do is sit! And sit you shall, and frighten away the birds that pull up the seeds. You can bang a tin and make a noise and perhaps you will earn your keep. Oh, why was I given this burden?" Father's voice rose to a shout, "Why didn't I have a proper son? Why did my wife die having this useless boy? Better they had both died!"

"Shush, shush," came a gentle voice from the corner of the hut. "Shanti is a blessing and honoured by the gods. His affliction is a test for him and for us. Through it, we will all be reborn into better lives. How we behave in this life affects us in the next. Remember this."

A bent old lady hobbled towards Shanti and patted his curly head. She looked sternly at Shanti's father and continued,

"My Shanti is a very special boy and Brahma, the supreme one, knows it."

Shanti looked gratefully up at her brown wrinkled face and she smiled down at him.

"Come, Shanti, come and have some supper and I'll sing you the songs I taught your mother."

Father's face creased in ill temper. After glowering at both of them, he angrily announced,

"I've had enough! I've had enough, I say! I've decided I want a new wife. I've been too long without one. I need to start looking now. Right away!"

"So be it," murmured the grandmother. "You start looking and I'll pray that you find a strong young woman!"

"Stronger than the last one," shouted Shanti's father, giving Shanti a furious look.

He then rummaged around the room, shoving clothes and blankets into a sack. Slinging the sack over his shoulder, he abruptly left. Shanti and his grandmother never laid eyes on him again.

When Shanti's father failed to return that night, grandmother sat outside the hut watching the path that led out from the village. After spending a week uselessly hoping that he would return, grandmother attempted to look after the paddy fields.

Shanti tried to help by pulling up weeds and waving away the birds. He banged two tins together, making a huge din. It was a hopeless task. The weeds grew and the cheeky birds disregarded the noise and tugged up the shoots. Eventually, grandmother had to beg her neighbours to help, and as the months went by the neighbours gradually took ownership of the fields. They sold the rice and kept most of the profits for themselves. They did look after Shanti and his grandmother, but stealthily the fields, once carefully tended by Shanti's family, were absorbed into those of the neighbours. Boundaries moved, ditches were filled in, fences pulled up and the neighbours' fields grew larger.

At first grandmother remonstrated with them. "Where is the money that you got for my rice?"

They refused to answer and grandmother wept and pulled her scarf over her face. Finally she stopped eating and speaking, and wouldn't rouse herself from her bed.

As grandmother lay on her side on her charpoy, not moving, Shanti tentatively shuffled over to her.

"Grandma, you must talk to me. Talk to me, grandma! Please, grandma!" He patted her with his thin little hand.

She half-turned her head, then pulling her scarf back over her face, turned to the wall. The neighbours came silently into the hut and stared at her. They spoke in hushed whispers.

"She'll have to go to the nuns. Put her in Sanjay's cart and take her to the nuns. They'll see to her."

"No! No! Please!" Shanti held on to the side of the bed. "I'll look after her; she's my grandma."

"Now, you know you can't look after her, Shanti. Let her go. It's for the best."

They prised his fingers off the frame of the bed and lifted the bed, with Shanti's grandmother on it, out of the door.

"But what will happen to me?" wailed Shanti, as his grandmother was lifted onto the cart.

"We'll look after you," somebody said, but Shanti hid his head in his arms and rocked himself backwards and forwards.

Next morning a family carrying cooking pots, mattresses and bundles of clothes moved into the hut. They ignored Shanti, and he retreated to a corner and sat there staring at them in absolute misery.

It was much later in the day, as the sun was setting, that there was a loud commotion outside. People were shouting and running about.

"The snake catcher is coming!"

"He's come for the big one."

"Quick, let's watch."

Small children excitedly grabbed each other's hands and ran after the adults.

Shanti hadn't seen any big snakes, though he had glimpsed some short thin ones in the fields. His curiosity gradually overcame his misery and he wearily pulled himself outside.

At the far side of the lane a small dark man with a large hooked nose and tiny close-together eyes was getting down from a donkey cart. From the cart he lifted out a large wicker basket and a bottle-shaped gourd with two bamboo pipes sticking out of it. One of the pipes had finger holes in it. The other one didn't. This was the snake charmer's musical instrument.

The villagers greeted him, formed a circle around him and waited expectantly. The children peeped round their legs. The man squatted on the ground and placed the basket in front of him. Slowly and carefully he lifted the basket's lid, tilted it to one side and began to play. His fingers played over the holes as he blew down into the pipe. The pipe emitted a strange discordant whine, which caused the little children to hurriedly clamp their hands over their ears.

Then, up, up from the basket came a slender black snake swaying from side to side. Its small eyes glittered and a forked tongue flicked in and out of its tight mouth. Taller and taller it grew, until Shanti thought it would fall out of the basket. He stared at it, almost mesmerised. The snake, which was facing him, seemed to stare back. Suddenly, without any warning, it dropped back into the basket. The snake charmer had abruptly stopped playing.

The crowd visibly relaxed. They clapped and threw some coins. The snake charmer put the lid back on the basket, lifted it onto the cart and went off with some villagers. A family had been terrified by a poisonous snake which had moved into the rafters of their hut. The snake charmer had been sent for to remove it. The rest of the crowd hesitated, then followed.

Shanti quickly scuttled after them; he was curious as to what would happen next. He positioned himself at the front of the crowd and watched.

Sitting himself down in the doorway of the family's large hut, the snake charmer once again played his pipe.

Nothing happened for a long time and the crowd, squashed together behind him, became impatient. Just as some people were about to wander off, something moved in the shadows.

"Ah!" the crowd murmured, their attention riveted once more. They all leaned forward and peered into the gloom. Down the far wall at the back of the hut, and emerging from the darkness, came a huge grey snake. It undulated across the floor, weaving its head from side to side.

The crowd gave a loud gasp of fright and quickly took a step backwards. Moving threateningly towards the snake charmer, the snake reared up in front of him. The crowd gave another gasp, clutched at each other and took another step back.

The snake charmer, unfazed by the snake's actions, played a strange, shrill tune on his pipe. Everyone stared transfixed at the big snake. Flattening itself on the ground, the snake appeared to be listening. Slowly, slowly, it lifted its head and then the front part of its body, and started to sway. Slowly, slowly, the snake charmer continued playing with one hand only. With the other he withdrew from his top garment a short stick with a V-shaped fork at one end. The snake swayed as if hypnotised by the music. Faster the music played, eventually descending into one loud, deafening drone. The snake dropped down onto the floor. Immediately, with a lightning pounce, the snake charmer leapt forward and pinned the head of the snake to the ground with his stick. The snake thrashed its body around in frenzy but, heave as it might, it couldn't escape. Two men brought a large plastic sheet from the cart. They held it over the trapped snake, then directed by the snake charmer they dropped it. Pulling the plastic under the snake they rolled it round its protesting body. Strong rope was tied around both ends of the plastic, with the V-shaped stick protruding from one end.

Someone brought the donkey and cart, and the snake was thrown over its side. Everyone applauded, patted the snake charmer's back, and he was given his payment. He counted the money quickly and, satisfied, he thrust it into his pocket. He was just about to get into his cart when he glanced down and noticed Shanti. Handing the donkey's reins to a person nearby, he approached Shanti and slyly prodded him with a bony finger.

"A snake boy," he hissed in his ear. "You have eyes like a snake, darting and watchful. You wriggle on the ground like a snake. I need someone to help me. It could be you, snake boy."

Shanti opened his eyes wide with alarm and shrank back. He turned to flee, but the crowd had closed in around him. Turning to the crowd, the snake charmer shouted in a loud voice.

"Who does this boy belong to? Where is his family?"

"He has no family," someone said.

"No, he hasn't. His father's gone away."

"His grandmother's gone away as well."

"He's got nobody." Everyone nodded at this.

Shanti gave a sob and covered his face with his hands as he felt himself being lifted up and put into the donkey cart.

"I'll look after him. Yes, he'll be well looked after by me," proclaimed the snake charmer to everyone.

"A good man. A fortunate boy," voiced the crowd to each other.

"No," whispered Shanti. "No!" The snake charmer jumped into the cart, caught hold of the donkey's reins and smacked the donkey with a stick.

Through the swirling dust and the cries of many children racing after them, Shanti was borne away. Behind him in the cart, the large snake heaved in its plastic prison.

3

Takshaka Bites

They had travelled some distance, neither of them speaking, when the snake charmer suddenly stopped the cart. He clambered round Shanti and attempted to heave the snake over the side, but it was too heavy for one person. After tugging at it uselessly for a few minutes the snake charmer snapped,

"Help me, you stupid, lazy boy."

Shanti grasped the end of the snake and tried to lift it. Whereupon the snake slipped out of his grasp and, despite being wrapped in plastic, wound itself around the legs of the snake charmer. He wobbled, lost his balance and fell out of the cart, with the snake landing on top of him.

Shanti fell backwards and couldn't move for hysterical laughter. He shoved his fist in his mouth but repeatedly shook with barely stifled snorts. Peering cautiously over the side of the cart, he saw that the snake charmer was now sitting on the snake, holding the head end in his two hands. Again Shanti had to smother his uncontrollable giggles and fall backwards.

The snake charmer, now in command of the situation, dragged the snake by its head to some distance away from the cart. He undid one end of the plastic and retreated quickly. The snake gradually emerged. It seemed to turn its head to stare at the snake charmer, then lay still in the hot sun. Backing away cautiously, the snake charmer leaned down and pulled the discarded stick and plastic sheeting slowly towards him. He gathered it up, walked backwards a few steps and pitched the sheeting into the cart. It landed on Shanti. The snake charmer climbed into the cart.

"Why did you let the snake go?" asked Shanti, after extricating himself.

"Oh! You've found your tongue at last, have you? I thought I'd picked up a deaf and dumb kid as well as a cripple." He looked at Shanti with mad, staring eyes.

"Takshaka!" he whispered menacingly. "I always free my captured snakes because, who knows, they might be the great snake god Takshaka. I always need to keep friends with him, or else ..."

"Or else what?" whispered Shanti, all giggles now gone.

"Or else he may pull me down to his underground kingdom. Down, down, under the earth. Don't you know anything?"

"I don't know anything about snakes," said Shanti fearfully.

"Well you'll soon learn. That's what you are here for, my little snake boy."

He hit the donkey with the stick and the cart trundled along the lane. It passed the paddy fields where the shoots of rice were growing tall, and trundled upwards towards some stony hills.

By a wet ditch, which threaded its damp way down to the paddy fields, the snake charmer yanked on the donkey's bridle and climbed out of the cart.

"We'll park here for the night." He proceeded to lift down the plastic and some poles from out of the cart. Finding a flat piece of ground, he splayed the poles out and tied them at the top, making a wigwam structure. He then tucked the plastic around it, fashioning a crude tent.

"Now you," he said moving back to the cart and lifting Shanti out, "can earn your keep. Get searching for frogs; the snakes are hungry."

"Frogs?"

"That's what I said. Frogs it is. Look under the stones, and when you catch them put them in this tin."

He flung Shanti a rusty tin, then poked around in the cart, looking for his cooking things. Shanti stared after him, not really understanding. After an impatient wave from the snake charmer he scuttled off to find some frogs.

There were some stones by the damp ditch.

"Turn them over, you useless boy," came the shout from the cart.

Shanti put the tin down beside him and carefully lifted up a stone. There was a little green frog, half-buried in the wet earth. Shanti quickly grabbed it, holding it tightly in his hand. He felt it squirming about, its small body desperately pushing at his clenched fingers. He dropped it into the tin. After turning over several other bigger stones, Shanti caught two more. Now he had three, and felt quite proud of himself. He put some twigs and leaves in the tin to make it like a home for the frogs. Sitting and watching them, Shanti hoped they liked their new house. The frogs didn't move; their golden eyes gazed unblinkingly at Shanti. Suddenly one gave a huge leap and cleared the side of the tin. Shanti just caught its little leg as it leapt to its freedom. He put it back and clutched the tin to his chest.

"How are you doing?" A shout from the snake charmer made Shanti start and look up.

"I've caught three. Is that enough?"

"Will do for now, bring them here."

Shanti shuffled over, carrying the tin carefully. The snake charmer snatched the tin from Shanti and emptied its contents into the snakes' basket. Shanti looked in horror as the little frogs huddled together in the middle of the coiled-up snakes.

"That'll do them." The snake charmer grinned at Shanti's shocked expression. "Now here's something for you." He handed him a tin plate with some beans and vegetables on it, and a grey-looking piece of naan bread. "Eat it up, then we'll bed down for the night. You'll not think of scarpering; I'm tying you to me with this." The snake charmer produced a rope. Tying one end around his waist and the other around Shanti's, he muttered:

"Move, and I'll know, and then you'll get a clobbering."

When Shanti had finished his food he lay down in the tent on the bare earth. The snake charmer threw a thin blanket over him and lay down beside him. It was hard and uncomfortable, and almost daylight before Shanti managed to drift off into a troubled sleep. Visions of little green frogs kept leaping before his eyes, and then a huge jaw would open wide and swallow them.

Next morning, when he was freed from the rope, Shanti tentatively lifted the lid of the snakes' basket: the frogs had gone. He gave a gasp of horror.

"Well, what did you expect?" asked the snake charmer, who was dismantling the tent. "That the snakes would keep them as pets? Food! That's what they were. Food! Now stop sniffling and get yourself into the cart."

The weeks went by. Shanti was given a tambourine to shake and a yellow turban to wear. The turban was too big and kept falling over one eye. He pushed it up and it fell over the other eye. He gave up trying to straighten it and sat there, banging the tambourine, wearing his lopsided turban and with a silly grin on his face.

They slowly travelled around the area, stopping at hamlets, villages and towns.

People seemed to know when the snake charmer was arriving. Running out of their houses to greet him, they would implore him to stop and put on a show or get rid of a harmful snake in the house.

It was great entertainment. Shanti gradually got to enjoy the feeling of anticipation and danger that accompanied the arrival of the little donkey cart.

One day the snake charmer obtained some new snakes. Carefully placing them in a box, he pulled from his pocket an open-weave white cloth. Shanti watched, transfixed, as he started to flick the cloth at the curled-up snakes. The snakes didn't react for a time. But then, curiosity overcoming them, they reared up out of the basket. The snakes stared eerily at the cloth, then abruptly sank their jaws into it. They reared back, their fangs caught in the open weave. With a sharp tug of the cloth, the snake charmer ripped their fangs out.

"You see, my friend," informed the snake charmer, pocketing the cloth and the now defunct fangs, "Snakes have long hollow teeth connected to little bags filled with poison. Once pulled, they start their wicked growing again. So keep on ripping them out. Rip them, before they rip into you, I say."

"What happens if they do rip into you?" asked a terrified Shanti.

"Tie a string around the bite, pronto!" The snake charmer grinned menacingly at Shanti. "Else you will turn blue, swell up, and then you're for it."

"For what?" Shanti's eyes were getting bigger and bigger.

"For the big pull down into the earth with Takshaka!" the snake charmer yelled, looking quite mad. "For death, you stupid boy!"

He paused for a moment, continuing in a confidential whisper,

"But I've never been bitten. I'm too sharp for old Takshaka. I've got his number!" He patted his long, bony nose with his finger. "As long as I let him go, he and I are mates. Mates!"

Shanti gave a shiver of horror.

The next day saw the donkey cart trundle into a small town. It was hot and steamy; the pavements shimmered in the white heat. The snake charmer and Shanti worked hard. They entertained the crowds all day, and Shanti scampered around, picking up the rupees that were flung in appreciation.

Feeling hot and tired, the snake charmer tied the donkey's reins to a fence. He and Shanti then went to eat at a small dingy café. They sat down at a table and a man brought them some food.

"How's business?" asked the owner of the café, who was a friend of the snake charmer.

"Not bad! Not bad! No thanks to this boy, though," nodding in Shanti's direction.

"He's along for the ride then?" laughed the café owner, revealing a mouthful of brown, betel-stained teeth.

"A ride that's going to get bumpy if he doesn't shape up."

Shanti looked forlornly at the two men. He thought he was shaping up. Now he was very good at catching frogs for the snakes, although he hated it. He played his tambourine enthusiastically, and he learned that if he whistled he could make the snakes lift themselves out of their basket. But there was no pleasing the snake charmer and he still tied Shanti up at night.

"Is it okay if we sleep round the back?"

"No problem. Tether the donkey to the post in the corner."

The snake charmer and his friend chatted and smoked. As Shanti's eyes were beginning to close he was yanked round to an outhouse and tied to the snake charmer. They both fell asleep.

All was dark and quiet, except for the rustlings of some small creatures, when Shanti abruptly woke up. He didn't move. He lay very still and opened his eyes wide to try and see in the silvery moonlight. Through the open door he saw a long shape sliding around the yard. Sometimes it reared up and swayed from side to side.

"Takshaka," thought Shanti, now rigid with fear. "It's Takshaka."

His big eyes followed the shadowy shape coming into the outhouse. It slithered onto his blanket. Shanti bit his lip and clenched his fist to stop himself from crying out. Takshaka came closer and closer, then started to slide across his chest. Shanti shut his eyes tightly. His nostrils were filled with an earthy, musty smell. He felt the heavy weight of the snake as it passed over him and on to the snake charmer. He was then shocked out of his wits by a piercing shriek.

"Ah!! I've been bitten!"

Shanti pulled himself upright and tugged at the rope around his waist. He dragged it off him and rolled over to the body on the floor beside him.

"Bitten! I've been bitten."

"Where? Where?" Shanti screamed in horror.

"My arm! My arm!" The snake charmer held it up and in the moonlight Shanti could see it was swelling up and turning blue.

Shanti grabbed at the rope and tugged it off the snake charmer. He then wound it around the bitten arm, pulling it as tightly as he could. By this time the snake charmer was gasping for breath and his eyes were rolling back in his head.

The café owner came running into the outhouse, woken up by the screaming.

"Snake!" shouted Shanti, yanking at the rope. "It was a snake! He's been bitten!"

The café owner yelled out to some men still asleep on the pavement outside.

"Rickshaw! Get a rickshaw. The snake charmer has been bitten!"

A man ran off and came back with a sleepy rickshaw wallah. The snake charmer was bundled into the rickshaw and rushed off to the hospital.

Shanti was left by himself in the outhouse, and somewhere, in there with him, was the venomous snake.

When all was quiet, it silently appeared again. Shanti sat up, but this time he wasn't frightened: he had more a feeling of expectation.

The snake's long coils rippled across the floor. Raising itself in front of him, it swayed from side to side.

"Takshaka," whispered Shanti. "Takshaka the snake god." Without knowing why, he nervously tapped his fingers together. The snake's eyes glittered and it swayed more and more. It performed a kind of dance: a snake dance for Shanti. Then abruptly it dropped to the ground and as Shanti ceased his tapping, the snake turned and slithered away.

Shanti sat there, unmoving. It was only when the first rays of the sun lightened the yard that he realised his predicament and, perhaps, his good fortune.

He was now completely alone.

Could he drive the donkey cart?

Could he be the snake charmer?

Could he do it all by himself?

4

Shanti Takes Charge

He stayed in the yard all the next day, waiting for news of the snake charmer. The café owner shook his head when Shanti asked how he was.

"Depends, he said, nodding knowingly. "It depends on the antidote. Did he get it in time, or has Takshaka got him?" He turned away to serve some customers, leaving Shanti none the wiser as to the snake charmer's fate.

The braying of the hungry donkey reminded him that there was work to be done. How to get onto the cart? The snake charmer had tied the tent poles to the side. By holding onto them Shanti swung himself up and over into the cart. He checked that the snakes were okay in their basket, then picked up a bunch of green leaves used to feed the donkey. Swinging himself down, he fed the donkey and shuffled round to the café to speak again to the owner.

"I'm taking the donkey and cart back on the road. I need to earn some money. I'll do some snake charming, then come back to see if the master is better."

He tried to sound confident and grown-up. The café owner looked down at Shanti and laughed,

"Make sure the donkey doesn't run away with you or the snakes don't decide to be your special necklace."

Shanti shuddered. "I'll be back. I'll be back soon." With a show of confidence he was far from feeling, he waved to the café owner, scuttled off to the cart, untied the donkey from the post, and clambered in.

He was now the master. Shanti felt elated. But he was too low in the cart and could hardly see where he was going. Spotting the plastic, he pulled it towards him, folded it over and sat on top of it. Holding the reins tightly and tapping the donkey with the stick, he excitedly set off.

At first the donkey walked steadily. However, sensing that its usual master wasn't in charge, it kept stopping to munch on weeds growing by the side of the road. Shanti yanked on the reins and whacked at the donkey. Whereupon the donkey paused in its meanderings, lifted up its head, gave a loud bray, then galloped off down the road like a racehorse. Shanti slid off the plastic and sprawled in the cart. The reins fell out of his hands and he hung on to the sides of the cart as the donkey hurtled along, scattering people, cows, hens and pigs. The cart balanced on two wheels, then tipped over onto the other two wheels. The donkey continually emitted the loud braying as if broadcasting its new freedom. Faster and faster it galloped. Shanti closed his eyes tightly as the cart swayed from side to side. People screamed and leapt for safety.

He was saved by the brave actions of a street food seller. Seeing the runaway donkey and realising that his stall was about to be demolished, he rushed forward into the road and grabbed the dangling reins. Pulling with all his strength, he yanked at the donkey. The donkey skidded round in circles and the man hung on. After nearly being throttled by the reins, the donkey gave up. It stood still, trembling all over, left in a state of donkey shock at its new-found boldness, which had now all gone. It gave a muffled cough and hung its head.

Shanti's shocked face appeared over the side of the cart.

"Is this your wretched donkey?" The man's stern face frowned at Shanti.

"Er, um. Yes it is."

"Well, just keep it under control." He whacked the donkey on the nose and stumped off to serve a group of grinning people.

Shanti tentatively gathered up the reins. Oh dear! The donkey had run away with him. He hoped that the snakes wouldn't decide to be his special necklace.

But from that time on, the donkey behaved itself and Shanti dawdled along, visiting the villages along the road. He didn't have a clue as to where he was going, and just wandered along from one place to the next. He had found the snake charmer's pipe in the cart, so could put on a performance. Catching poisonous snakes was something he avoided doing. Shanti was much too frightened of something going wrong. With his earned rupees he bought hay for the donkey and small eggs for the snakes. He also caught insects and small mice. He never watched as the snakes devoured their food. Seeing a small mouse tail disappearing down the throat of the largest snake had put him off looking forever.

One night as he was camping by the side of the road and contemplating making a return journey to enquire after the snake charmer, something occurred to change everything.

He had just settled down to rest, when he heard a rickshaw pull up next to him. The plastic sheets were torn off his tent and there stood the snake charmer in a terrible fury. He shook his fists at Shanti and screamed at him,

"Thief! You ungrateful boy! Didn't I save you when nobody wanted you? Didn't I feed and look after you? And what do you do when I'm ill? Steal! Steal my cart! My donkey! My snakes!"

The snake charmer leapt on Shanti and pummelled him.

"Get out! Get out of my tent and scram," he roared at him.

"But I was coming back," moaned a shocked Shanti. "I didn't know what had happened to you. I had to look after ..."

But he said no more because the snake charmer punched him on the head and Shanti rolled backwards on the floor.

When he came to, everything had gone and he had been left, covered in dust, at the side of the road. He pulled himself upright and found that he was staring at the concerned face of a boy some years older than himself.

"Are you okay?" the boy asked anxiously. "What's your name?"

"Shanti. It's Shanti."

5

Hijacked

I saw what happened," the boy said. "We'd stopped the truck and when I got out I saw a man thumping you, then riding off in a donkey cart."

Truck, what truck? Shanti rubbed his bruised face.

"I've been helping two men load their truck. See, it's over there. They're giving me a lift to the city. I've got an uncle who's got a job for me. Are you feeling okay now? Why did that man hit you and why can't you walk?"

"He thought I'd stolen his cart," replied Shanti mournfully. "But I was looking after it for him. I've been working for him for a long time since my grandma left." Shanti stifled a sob. "My legs have always been like this, ever since I was born."

"What will you do now?"

"I don't know." Shanti bit his lip and frowned. Embarrassed, he attempted to shuffle away.

"Now look here, Shanti. My name is Rajiv. I could hide you under the lorry and you could come to the city and find some work." He patted Shanti's arm reassuringly. "I'll tie you under the lorry on a ledge. Lots of people secretly travel that way."

"On a ledge! I might fall off," said Shanti in horror.

"No, you'll be safe. I've travelled that way once."

Not having any other idea of what to do, Shanti rather reluctantly agreed to Rajiv's plan.

25

Whilst the men were having a rest, Rajiv sneaked Shanti round to the side of the lorry and showed him the ledge between the cabin and the trailer.

"Crawl in, I'll cover you with sacks and tie you on."

Shanti peered worriedly under the lorry but, pushed by Rajiv, he crawled underneath and pulled himself onto the ledge. Rajiv got some sack and a rope from the trailer and tied him tightly.

"It's not too far. You'll be safe. Don't worry."

Shanti managed a panicky smile.

"Thanks, Rajiv. Thanks."

There was a shout from the men. Rajiv gave Shanti a conspiratorial wink and left. Shanti heard him climbing the steps into the lorry's cabin.

The engine revved. Deafened by the noise and nearly suffocated by diesel fumes, Shanti gave himself up to his fate. He shoved his fingers in his ears and thought of his grandmother. What would she think of him now? Where were the gods to take care of him?

The truck roared off. It lurched and bounced over the side of the road until it reached the tarmac. Shanti was heaved about, but Rajiv's ropes held him firm. He was away to the big city and to whatever awaited him.

Except, the lorry never managed to reach the big city because a disastrous event overtook them.

They were moving slowly up a steep hill; Shanti was glad of the respite. When the lorry was moving fast, he felt as if all his bones were being shaken loose. They had reached the top and were about to descend the other side, when the lorry came to an abrupt halt. Loud, strident voices were yelling something. Shanti lifted his head to hear better.

"Out you get, else we'll drag you out!"

To Shanti's increasing alarm he heard the lorry's door bang open and the noise of the two drivers being pulled to the ground.

"Get up and walk to those trees!"

Straining to see from under the lorry, Shanti saw four legs being marched away by six other legs.

His heart almost stopped when somebody whispered in his ear.

"Hijacked! Thieves are stealing the lorry. Quick, Shanti! We must move quickly!"

Rajiv pulled at the rope, threw off the sack and yanked Shanti out from the ledge. He then pushed and heaved him up into the cab of the lorry. Climbing over him, he seated himself in the driver's seat and grasped the wheel. Shanti stared at him, and his breath came in short gasps.

"What are you doing, Rajiv? Do you know what you are doing?"

"Hang on and shut up!"

Rajiv reached down, released the handbrake, and with the cabin doors still swinging open the lorry started to move down the hill. Shanti gave a little scream, gripped the sides of the seat and hung on. This was much more serious than the donkey cart.

He was conscious of loud shouts behind them, but they faded into the distance as the lorry gathered speed. The doors banged backwards and forwards as they charged down the hill.

Rajiv's feet couldn't reach the pedals or the foot brake; he just held on to the steering wheel and wildly careered round the corners. They barely missed a bus, which honked its horn in fury, and all the time the lorry went faster.

Shanti closed his eyes, but quickly opened them again as the lorry banged into a boulder at the side of the road. The lorry swerved but miraculously managed to keep up its headlong sprint. An unfortunate aged hen was squashed flat and her companions scattered, when the lorry reached a particularly bad bend.

Rajiv just managed to keep control as the lorry screeched round the corner. Suddenly there was a frightening crunching noise. The back of the lorry broke free from its couplings, careered into a field and promptly turned over. The cab, released from the weight of the trailer, almost took flight. Off it soared, like an aeroplane. Desperately, Rajiv grabbed the handbrake and pulled on it. The cab completed a mad squealing circle in the middle of the road. There was a loud bang as one of the tyres burst and the cab tilted drunkenly backwards, then continued limping slowly down the hill. Slower and slower it went, until it eventually gave a shudder and came to stop near a roadside café.

Shanti was in total shock. He couldn't move or say anything. Rajiv, however, was in a state of wild exhilaration. He laughed madly when he saw Shanti's face.

"Come on, it wasn't that bad. Don't you think I'm a brilliant driver? I should be in films."

Shanti stared at him in disbelief.

"Brilliant driver! We could have crashed and been killed!"

"Well, we didn't! And we escaped from the robbers. You, my friend, are a little scaredy cat." He gave Shanti a poke with his finger and a crazy grin. "Come on, we'll go into that café, have some food and see if we can sort something out." He pulled down a flap over the mirror in the cabin and drew out a handful of rupees. "I think we've earned these!"

Shanti was still trembling when Rajiv lifted him down from the cab.

Rajiv laughed hysterically when he saw the state of the lorry.

"No use to the robbers now," he muttered to himself. "No use to anyone." And louder, "Come on, Shanti, let's eat."

Men stared curiously as Rajiv and Shanti entered the café, but after whispered comments to their companions, they disregarded them. Rajiv helped Shanti onto a chair and went to the counter to order.

After eating steaming platefuls of chicken curry, mopped up with light floury chapattis, a now somewhat relaxed Shanti sat back and grinned at Rajiv.

"I know a brilliant driver," he said.

"And it's me?" asked Rajiv, lifting his eyebrows.

"Yes, it's you, Rajiv. You are the best."

"All set up for Bollywood, Shanti?"

Shanti laughed out loud.

"Yes! Yes! Yes!"

"I'll be a Bollywood stuntman," boasted Rajiv. "I've got what it takes."

"Yes, you have," agreed Shanti. He felt so relieved they hadn't died that he was prepared to tell Rajiv anything.

"Now wait here for a moment," Rajiv got down from his chair. "I've just got something to sort out."

Shanti watched in admiration as his friend moved confidently around the room, talking to the men. Most of them listened and then shook their heads, but there was one young man who appeared interested. He and Rajiv spoke for a few moments, he nodded and Rajiv reached into his pocket and handed him some notes.

"Well, that's settled then, Shanti. We're off to the city on a motorbike and you're coming." Rajiv nodded in the direction of the young man. "He says you'd better hold on tight."

Outside the café was a powerful Royal Enfield motorbike. The biker had put on his helmet and was already revving the engine when Shanti and Rajiv appeared.

"Climb on," he yelled over his shoulder.

Shanti looked at Rajiv in some alarm, but Rajiv heaved him up and squashed him behind the driver. He then swung himself onto the bike and sat behind Shanti.

"Hold onto the man, Shanti."

Shanti grabbed the man around the waist and Rajiv held onto him.

Zoom! They were off. Leaning at crazy angles, they hurtled round corners and overtook every living thing on the straight stretches.

Again Shanti's terror made him close his eyes tightly. He buried his face in the man's back and held on.

The engine throbbed on his poor legs and the speed and the leanings made him feel ... fantastic.

He was flying, swimming, running and jumping, all merging together. He'd never before felt such an amazing feeling of freedom.

"Keep going! Keep going!" he sang to himself. The beautiful motorbike sleekly responded. Shanti forgot about his legs; he lost himself in the joy of the power.

"Keep going! Keep going!"

Swaying, roaring down the road, Shanti was in heaven.

"Keep going! Keep on for ever!"

He opened his eyes and saw the landscape blur by. Trees, houses, people became bands of changing light and colour.

He felt held in a safe bubble where nothing could touch or harm him. This was truly magic.

But all too soon the bike began to slow down, and with a muffled roar from the engine it turned into the forecourt of a petrol station.

"Need more fuel," said the man, getting off. "And I need a leak. Wait here, you two." He stomped off towards the services.

Shanti turned his head to look at Rajiv and was about to say how wonderful the ride was, when he noticed the expression on Rajiv's face. Shanti followed the direction of the look, and what he saw made him gasp with alarm.

The road in front had a rope across it. Policemen were checking the cars and there, at the side of the road, stood the two lorry drivers whom Rajiv had helped. They were looking intently at anyone leaving the garage.

"I can't go with you," muttered Rajiv. "I can't. I wrecked the lorry. I'll be caught and gaoled for stealing the lorry and for wrecking it."

"But you escaped! You could have been kidnapped, Rajiv."

"Yes, but who'll believe me, Shanti? Better we part, little friend."

He got down from the bike and grinned at Shanti's worried face.

"Don't worry. I'm a survivor. Didn't you say I was brilliant?"

"Yes, Rajiv. You are the best, but what are you going to do?"

"Hitch a lift on one of the lorries in the same way that you did."

Rajiv leaned over and squeezed Shanti's shoulder, then walked towards some parked lorries. He turned once to wave at Shanti, then disappeared.

The man came back.

"Where's your mate?"

"He had to go somewhere," mumbled Shanti. "He met a friend."

"Well, I can't wait for him. I'll fill up, then we'll be off."

He filled the tank with petrol, paid a man at a kiosk, and then manoeuvred the bike towards the police cordon.

The two lorry drivers barely looked at them, they dropped the rope and the motorbike roared off with Shanti holding on, his face wet with tears.

6

Shanti the Hero

On the outskirts of a large town the motorbike slowed down and made its way towards a large lake which had steps leading down to the water. "This is where we part company, mate."

The driver stopped the engine, got off, helped Shanti down, got back on and drove away.

Shanti looked round in bewilderment. All around him people were bathing in the lake. Some were performing rituals to their gods, asking for comfort or for help. Wreaths of marigolds and jasmine floated by. Priests clambered up and down the steps, filling large brass pots with water and pouring it over the many pilgrims needing its blessing. The lake was holy, and people came from many miles away to make a pilgrimage to it.

Shanti crawled to the steps and gazed at the water. Covering his face with his hands, he lay on his side and was filled with despair.

Much later, when much of the excited babble of the people had abated, Shanti sat up. He stared at the black, glittering water of the lake. He was tired, so tired. Darkening ripples made small wavy circles which whirled around, then floated away. Shanti's eyes were drooping shut when, emerging from the centre of one of the circles, he vaguely caught sight of a long sinewy shape. "Takshaka! The snake god!" he murmured.

It moved its head as if beckoning Shanti to follow. Staring in disbelief, Shanti began to shuffle down the lakeside steps. As if in a trance he reached the water's edge and slipped quietly into the lake. The warm muddy waters closed over him as he floated away, his head disappearing beneath the lake's surface. "I'm coming, Takshaka. Take me with you."

A strong hand grabbed at his hair and hauled him upwards. Coughing and choking, he was dragged back to the steps and laid on his stomach. His poor legs twisted beneath him as he felt a weight pushing up and down on his back. Turning his head to the side, he vomited lake water all over someone's sandals.

"He'll survive!"

"The gods be praised."

"He's meant to stay with the living for some time yet."

Distant voices drifted over Shanti as he lay with his face in the dirt.

"Come on, try and sit up now, young man."

A kindly voice roused Shanti and he felt someone lift him upright. He opened his eyes and stared straight into the gentle face of an old man who was leaning over him.

"You're shivering. Put my shawl around you and rest a moment." He placed a shawl around Shanti's shoulders. "There now, can you follow me?"

Shanti nodded immediately.

"Make way, everyone!" Waving his arms, the old man cleared a path through the crowds and helped Shanti up the steps. He then led the way to a row of huts. At the first one he stopped and banged on the door. A woman opened it and gazed down at Shanti.

"What's this you've brought me, baba?"

"He fell in the lake and needs some dry clothes."

"Fell in the lake!" The woman sounded amazed at Shanti's mishap. "Well, come in then, come in."

She bustled around at the back of the hut and brought out a shirt and some shorts.

"They belong to my son, but now they are much too small. He can have these."

She helped Shanti out of his wet rags and pulled on the shirt and shorts.

"A bit big. But as he doesn't stand, the shorts can't fall down." She gave a little laugh. "Here's your shawl, baba."

The elderly man looked approvingly at Shanti's new attire.

"Can he stay here for the night? I'll come back tomorrow."

"For one night then, baba," the woman agreed. Baba nodded his head and left.

The woman looked at Shanti with concern.

"How did you manage to fall in the lake and where's your family?"

"I don't know. I don't know. My legs... I must have slipped, and I have no family," whispered Shanti sadly.

"Well, never you mind. I'll get you some supper and you'll feel better."

She busied herself in a small kitchen and brought out some hot samosas and curried vegetables.

Shanti smiled at her gratefully,

"Thank you, thank you."

"Well, eat up and when you've finished you can sleep in that corner over there. You'll be out of the way when my family comes back."

Shanti ate everything he was given. He shuffled over to the corner, curled up and immediately dozed off.

Later that night he was vaguely aware of people quietly settling down to sleep near him and hushed voices murmuring softly.

Early in the morning, just as the first dawn light was creeping into the hut, Shanti opened his eyes. Something had roused him. Familiar rustlings and stirrings were coming from the hut's ceiling. He peered upwards. A long winding shape was making its way down to where various bodies were slumbering.

"No!" screamed Shanti at the top of his voice. "No!"

The family started up in confusion. The snake hurriedly retreated back into the roof, but not before everyone had seen it. They all fled outside in a panic. All except for Shanti. He pulled himself to the centre of the hut and sat there very still.

"Come away! Come out!" urgent voices called to him.

"Look out! He'll bite!"

They all stared through the doorway at Shanti. He shook his head and refused to move.

Shanti had no snake charmer pipes, but whilst he had lived with the snake charmer he had learned some special tricks.

Sitting absolutely still, he waited. Whilst he waited he pursed his lips and emitted a shrill sound. Patiently, he sat there whistling. The family, transfixed, watched from the doorway.

Down from the ceiling came a long poisonous snake. Never taking his eyes off it, Shanti's whistle became louder and more melodious. The snake reared up in front of him and swayed. Mirroring the snake, Shanti also swayed and his whistling sounded like a lively dance. Abruptly he stopped. The whistle then restarted as one long wailing note.

Flattening itself on the floor, the snake slid towards Shanti, its head weaving from side to side and its huge fangs showing.

There was a sudden pause and the people watching all held their breath.

Suddenly Shanti leapt forward. He grabbed the snake behind its head and pinned it to the floor. The snake reacted in fury to its capture, lashing out violently with its long body.

"Get me a blanket! Anything!" yelled Shanti.

Somebody threw him a cloth. Holding the snake's head down with one hand, Shanti snatched at the cloth. He cautiously moved his hand back a little way, and as the snake reared its head he pulled the cloth under and twisted it round and round its head.

"Rope!!" he screamed.

Somebody threw in a length of rope. Holding one end between his teeth, he slid the rest of the rope under the cloth and then bound it tighter and tighter. All the time the body of the snake was frenziedly heaving about.

On seeing that Shanti had covered and secured the snake's head, several men now rushed into the hut to help.

"Quick! I need a bigger cloth."

A blanket was found and wrapped round the body of the snake. A second rope secured it. The bundled-up snake now lay still.

An exhausted Shanti looked up at the admiring faces of the people and an excited babble of voices deafened him.

"Who is this boy?"

"He was wonderful!"

"What bravery!"

"What shall we do with the snake now?"

To the last question, Shanti answered,

"Help me carry it to a place far away from people. Then we must let it go."

He looked down contemplatively at the undulating bundle. "All life is sacred, even that of a poisonous snake. My grandma taught me this. Takshaka the snake god knows when one of his own is harmed."

The people nodded their heads in agreement at this and looked respectfully at Shanti.

Two men lifted the snake onto a handcart and, with Shanti helped up and seated next to the snake, they pushed the handcart down the lane.

Once away from the people's dwellings, they lifted the snake down, undid the ropes and retreated behind the handcart.

Eventually the snake emerged from the cloth. Seemingly in shock from its dramatic capture, it lay still for a while. The men, becoming impatient, lobbed a few pebbles at it. With the realisation that it was now free, the snake slowly dragged itself to the rough grass by the side of the track and disappeared.

On their return to the hut they were met by a noisy welcome. Women had begun preparing food, and several men were sitting and playing their drums and tambourines. Someone had lit a fire. Skinny, bright-eyed children were dancing around it, waving their hands in the air and pretending to bite each other like snakes.

They all cheered when they saw the handcart with Shanti on it. A mat was placed in front of the first hut. Shanti was made to sit in the centre of it. Some of the men sat down beside him. Flat leaves were used as plates, as the women scurried about, serving everyone steaming rice, vegetables and curried goat meat.

Shanti was overwhelmed by the attention he received. The mother gave a speech telling of his bravery. Her sons shouted in loud agreement and thumped Shanti on the back. The children took to creeping up on Shanti and stroking and patting him.

For the first time in his short life he was admired and applauded. Smiling and nodding, he ate everything handed to him, until he felt stuffed with food and happiness.

Some time later, baba appeared and was told of Shanti's bravery.

"He will stay with us," said the woman. "He can help the men with the puppets."

"Shanti! Shanti! Come and play with us," the children pleaded. "Shanti! Shanti!"

7

The Xylophone

T he family that Shanti had now joined was an extended family of puppeteers. The men travelled around the area in a pick-up truck, putting on performances. The women usually stayed at home, caring for the children and making and repairing the large puppets.

When the old man had listened to the tale of bravery and Shanti's inclusion in the group, he quickly made a decision: one that would cause him to delay his planned journey.

"If Shanti stays with you he must contribute to the family," he announced. "I will take it upon myself. He shall play an instrument. I will take it upon myself to make one and teach him how to play it." He patted Shanti on the head. "I expect you to be an excellent student."

"Oh, I will be," answered Shanti fervently. "But what can I play, baba?"

"Leave that to me. Tonight I make it. Tomorrow we start."

"Make what? Make what?"

Smilingly baba said, "Patience, patience, Shanti. Music making starts with patience."

Next morning, true to his word, the old man brought Shanti his musical instrument. When baba placed it in front of him, Shanti stared at it with disappointment.

"What's this, baba? How can this make music? It looks like a little wooden gate."

The old man ignored him. He squatted down facing Shanti, and handled the xylophone tenderly. He unclipped two small wooden mallets from the sides of the xylophone and proceeded to play.

Tapping the slats of wood with one mallet, then two, he made sounds of bubbling clear waters and raindrops splashing in puddles. Shanti's attention was immediately caught; he listened intently, his mouth opening in wonder.

"That's beautiful, baba, beautiful. I want to play like you, baba. Can you teach me?"

So the lessons began. Mornings and afternoons were spent watching, listening and practising. Under the expert tuition of baba, Shanti concentrated hard. He played the xylophone every moment of his spare time. Baba and the family looked on in satisfaction at his rapid progress.

After three months had gone by baba quietly said,

"You have done well, Shanti. I'm very pleased with you. You are going to be an excellent musician." He paused, then continued, "Keep on practising and experimenting. Above all, listen to the sounds around you and within you. As you speak to your xylophone, make it answer back to you."

"But we haven't finished our lessons yet, baba?"

"Yes we have, Shanti. Now it's up to you and I must move on. I stopped here for longer than I intended because you needed me. Now you do not need me any more."

"But I do! I do, baba! I do need you." Shanti's voice rose loud in panic and desperation.

The old man looked at him with love and compassion.

"Listen, Shanti, because one day you will be old like me. There comes a time when work has finished, children have gone and wives do not need you. Then something tells you that you must begin the journey that will lead you to the supreme one: your maker. The blessed enlightened one. That is the journey I am on and that I must continue now."

"But you have nothing to take on your journey," Shanti wailed.

"There's no point in carrying possessions, Shanti. They just get in the way. We brought nothing into this world and we can take nothing from it when we die."

"You're not going to die, baba." Shanti sounded more frantic.

"No, not yet. I still have a long way to go," said baba calmly. "But," and he looked intently at Shanti, "I can't take you with me. I must do this alone, Shanti. Besides," he continued, "you, like everyone else, have your own journey to complete. Now stay with the people here, they are good people and they will take care of you."

"Baba! Oh, baba!" cried Shanti.

The old man bent over and for a few seconds held Shanti's face in his hands.

"Live for your music, Shanti. It's a blessing not given to everyone."

He closed his eyes for a brief second and then he left.

Shanti watched his slight, bent figure walk away, and then burst into sobs, stifling them with difficulty when he realised they were to no effect. His baba had left, leaving him with two priceless gifts: one, the ability to create beautiful music, and the other an insight into the wisdom that can come when life is reaching its close.

8

Puppeteers and Disasters

Once the family saw that baba had gone and that Shanti could now play the xylophone beautifully, they included him in their activities. Mornings would be spent working in the few fields the family owned, rehearsing the show, and other odd jobs. Much care was spent on an old pick-up truck, used for transporting the show to various locations. The men paid special attention to recharging the spare battery, as it was necessary to have bright lights on the stage. All this would be accompanied by endless cups of tea whilst sorting out the squabbles and needs of the innumerable lively children.

In the late afternoon the truck was packed with all the puppets and props. The men would jump aboard and drive to the surrounding villages or into the city. After carefully choosing a spot to perform, usually at the side of a main square or, after negotiations, at the front of a big hotel, there was a bustle of activity. The puppet theatre was erected. The puppets were laid out behind the theatre, ready for action. A long cable was connected from the truck's battery to the front of the theatre to power the spotlights. A bench was placed behind the theatre for the puppeteers to stand on. They then took up their positions, holding the strings of the first performing puppets. A red velvet curtain, trimmed with gold, concealed all these happenings from the audience.

It must have been the puppeteers' shouts or the sight of the old pick-up truck that alerted the children. They raced along to secure the best positions right behind the anchored spotlights. There they sat in eager anticipation, arms around each other and chattering like little birds.

More and more people arrived, mothers with babies and dads holding toddlers. Grandmothers, grandfathers, aunts and uncles, all settled themselves cross-legged on the ground behind the children. Some people stood at the side, mainly groups of giggling boys and girls. They slyly eyed one another and pretended not to be interested in the show; secretly they were aware of everything.

At a signal from the chief puppeteer, the curtain was pulled open. It was accompanied by cheers and claps from the crowd. Then everyone waited in excited suspense for the show to begin.

Shanti sat with two men at the side of the stage. One man played a pipe, the other a drum, and Shanti his xylophone.

Onto the stage came three splendidly dressed kings, looking very dignified. Wobbling before them appeared a rather plump dancing girl. The puppeteers made her wriggle and jiggle. Her bare tummy shook round and round. The three kings watched entranced. One of them couldn't contain his excitement and joined her in the dance. Suddenly his head broke loose from his body and shot up in the air. One of the kings caught it. The musicians played faster and faster, though Shanti was laughing so much he could hardly keep pace. The audience hooted and jeered, as the headless king chased after the dancing girl and the other two kings hastily followed, carrying his head.

Next came a snake charmer whose giant cobra leapt out of a basket and pursued him round and round the stage. There was huge applause for this scene, though it was Shanti's least favourite.

The last act was an acrobat riding a horse that had real flames flaring from its hooves. Shanti pounded on his xylophone and stared in disbelief. How did the puppeteers do that? Surely the flames would set fire to the strings? But no! The horse galloped about and the acrobat did amazing gymnastics. He leapt on and off the horse, stood on his head in the saddle and then turned somersaults. He ended up racing behind the horse, hanging on to its tail.

All too soon the show was over, but before the audience could depart they were gently hassled into putting a contribution into a collection box. The children slipped away, but the adults generously donated their rupees and soon the box was overflowing.

The theatre was quickly dismantled and put back in the pick-up truck. The cable was disconnected and everyone, hugely satisfied, drifted home.

Shanti adored being part of the puppeteers' family and travelling in the truck. He had now been with them for several months. He'd fixed a string onto his xylophone so that he could carry it on his back. His arms were then left free to propel himself around. He loved the different performances, especially the one that told of the love of Rama and Sita and the defeat of Ravana, the demon king. A distant memory of his grandmother telling him that story floated around his head. The headless king made him choke with laughter, and he delighted in seeing the enthralled looks on the faces of the children as they followed every detail of the entertainment.

It was too good to last. One evening the lights went out. The performance was being staged in one of the city's squares. One minute the dancing girl was wobbling her dance, the next minute total darkness. Everyone waited for the lights to go back on, but instead there was the sound of the pick-up truck's engine being revved. The two musicians immediately leapt up.

"The truck!" they yelled. "Someone's stealing the pick-up!"

They abandoned their instruments and raced off round to the back of the theatre. Shanti scrabbled after them. What he saw shocked him. Three youths had disconnected the cable, slammed down the bonnet and, because the engine had been left running to power the lights, were now attempting to drive it off.

The two musicians flung themselves at the truck and yanked the driver's door open. One of the men fell off the pick-up as it screeched out of the square. The truck careered down a side street for a few yards, with the other musician hanging on to the door and pulling at the steering wheel. Swerving from side to side, the truck hit a deep rut, tilted over and stopped.

The rest of the puppeteers caught up and dragged the youths out of the cab. They were thrown on the floor and soundly beaten. Their hands and feet were bound with bits of cable and they were left at the side of the road. A breathless Shanti arrived when all the action was finished.

The puppeteers were very angry. "Stay here and watch these villains, Shanti," ordered the chief puppeteer. "We'll quickly pack up before all our other stuff is stolen, and then get the police."

The men rushed off and Shanti was left looking at the three battered bodies. One of them turned his blood-smeared face and stared at Shanti.

"Rajiv!" gasped Shanti, horrified. "Rajiv! I thought you'd got a job with your uncle."

"No job! No uncle!" mumbled Rajiv through swollen lips and a missing tooth.

"Shanti, untie me. I'm for prison when the police come. It'll be the end of me." Rajiv spat a mouthful of blood into the dirt. "You can say I escaped."

"But I can't, Rajiv! I can't! These are my family now."

"I helped you, didn't I, Shanti? Now it's your turn."

Shanti shuffled reluctantly towards Rajiv. He pulled the knots loose around Rajiv's wrists, then sat back, horrified at what he'd done. He was even more horrified when Rajiv undid the cable around his ankles and proceeded to untie his two accomplices.

"Not those two! Only you, Rajiv!"

"These are my mates, can't leave them behind. Thanks, Shanti, now we are quits."

"Rajiv!! What will I do?"

"You'll get by; someone else will come along, Shanti."

The gang scarpered, leaving a terrified Shanti behind. He sat petrified with fear, wondering what the consequences would be for him. He was not long in finding out.

The men returned, found the gang had gone, and Shanti sitting and hiding his face in his hands.

"What's happened?"

"How did they escape?"

"Are you okay, Shanti?"

The chief puppeteer walked over to Shanti and shook his shoulder.

"Where are they, Shanti? Answer me, Shanti. What's the matter with you?"

Still nothing came from Shanti, and there was a sudden realisation on the part of the puppeteer.

"Did you untie them?" A pause of disbelief ensued. "You did, didn't you? You untied them."

The man hit Shanti, a resounding whack across his head. The rest of the men stared grimly at him.

"Why did you let them go?"

"He was my friend," sobbed Shanti.

All the puppeteers now surrounded Shanti, who cried uncontrollably.

"Those youths were wicked, Shanti. Don't you realise that? We could have been left with no pick-up, no transport. What would we have done then? And they will do it again. They will steal someone else's truck or car, and who knows what will happen?" He smacked Shanti again. "It was a stupid thing to do, Shanti. What would baba think? We took you in. We looked after you, Shanti. We were wrong to do so."

The chief puppeteer paused. "We don't want you with us now. You let us down, Shanti. Take your xylophone and go. The bus station is round the corner. Catch a bus back to your village."

All the men looked contemptuously at Shanti, threw him his xylophone and, as an afterthought, some rupees, then left to inspect the truck.

"I have no village." Shanti's plaintive cry followed them. They ignored him. Helped by a growing audience of curious men, they heaved the truck out of the deep rut and loaded it up.

Shanti was dimly aware of the sound of the pick-up driving away, leaving him behind. He stared uncertainly about him, avoiding several hostile expressions. Realising that nobody cared, he clutched at his xylophone and with shaking fingers lifted it over his shoulder. It was a forlorn little figure that slowly shuffled down to the bus station.

9

Ashiq and the Beggar Boys

At the bus station there were people standing with bags and parcels, waiting for their buses. Shanti dodged them and scuttled into a corner where he tried to hide away.

Devastated that he had once more been abandoned, he again had no idea what to do. Hugging his xylophone to him, he closed his eyes in despair.

"Rajiv! Rajiv!" he murmured to himself. "Why did it have to be you?"

A light touch on his shoulder startled him. He opened his eyes and was confronted by the pale face, surrounded by frizzy black hair, of a boy somewhat older than himself. The boy was sitting in a low, box-like wooden truck.

"I saw you come into the station. Your legs are bad. What's the matter? Are you okay?"

Shanti looked at the sympathetic face.

"No, I'm not okay," he replied miserably. I've been stupid, so stupid."

"Well, tell me about it, that's if you want to."

So Shanti told Ashiq, for that was the boy's name, all that had happened.

"And I've let baba down." Shanti was distraught. "Do you think I was very wicked, Ashiq?"

"No, not wicked, just a bit silly," smiled Ashiq. "You had a hard decision to make, Shanti. You did what you felt was right at the time." He nodded reassuringly. "Now what are you going to do?"

Shanti gazed at the busy scene of the bus station.

"I don't know. I really don't."

"Well, you could come back with me, but you'll have to be able to earn money. See, I live with these other kids. We work for this man we call uncle. In return for all we earn he looks after us, gives us food and somewhere to sleep. Some of us beg. Some of us entertain. It's okay."

"What do you do, Ashiq?"

"I'm an entertainer," said Ashiq proudly. "Just you watch this."

Ashiq somersaulted out of his truck. Shanti stared at Ashiq's legs, amputated above his knees. He continued to watch in amazement as Ashiq balanced all of his body on one strong hand and then on the other. He twirled round on his head and finished off by spinning round on his back.

Shanti, with several other onlookers, clapped enthusiastically.

"Now, what can you do, Shanti?"

Lifting his xylophone off his back and placing it carefully on the ground, Shanti then unclipped the two mallets. He thought for a few minutes, gazed unseeingly at the crowds, and played a plaintive little tune that reflected all the sadness he was feeling. Ashiq nodded understandingly.

"You'll do. That was good. Now follow me, Shanti boy."

So the two crippled boys left the bus station, one pushing himself along in a battered wooden truck and the other shuffling quickly behind.

After negotiating several busy road crossings, much to Shanti's relief they turned into a small side street. At the end of a long wall was an old wooden door. On reaching it, Ashiq pushed it open and propelled his truck through. Shanti followed, somewhat apprehensively.

They were in a messy yard strewn with garbage. There was a low concrete shack with a concrete veranda running the length and around the side of it. Sitting or standing on the veranda were about eight scruffy young boys. Their voices rose into a loud confusing babble when they saw Ashiq and Shanti.

"You've found another!" yelled one of the boys. "Lucky him! You'll be uncle's best boy, Ashiq!"

Ashiq ignored him. "Come round the side with me, Shanti, and I'll tell uncle you're here."

Shanti nervously followed Ashiq to a door at the side of the shack and Ashiq banged on it

A huge man with bleary red eyes and a scraggy black beard opened it. He frowned at Ashiq and squinted sideways at Shanti, who avoided looking at him and tried to hide behind Ashiq.

"What do you want?"

"I found Shanti at the bus station. He can make good music, uncle. Can he stay?"

The big man leered at them both, causing Shanti to involuntarily shudder.

"If he can earn me rupees he can stay forever," growled uncle. "Collect him a bed roll and sort him out."

He banged the door shut, then quickly opened it again.

"And where's your takings?"

"Here." Ashiq rummaged in his top and pulled out a handful of rupees.

"That all?" The man reached down and pawed around Ashiq's shirt. Satisfied he'd got everything, he went back into his shack, slamming the door behind him. Ashiq grinned at Shanti,

"Well, that's okay, Shanti boy. You're in." He picked up a grubby, rolled-up blanket from the side of the door, and trundled his truck around to the front of the veranda. Manoeuvring it to the end of the veranda, Ashiq threw the bed roll down. Shanti hurriedly followed him, then sat with his back pressed up against the far wall, staring at the beggar boys. With big round eyes, they all stared back at him. A noise from the door of the shack suddenly distracted them. A woman's voice called out. The boys then pushed and shoved their way into the shack. They all sat in a long row on the stone floor and waited. Ashiq and Shanti, coming in last, sat at the end.

Shanti cautiously looked around at the bedlam surrounding him. Some boys couldn't control their poor twitching limbs. Others had a missing leg or a missing arm. One boy had dreadfully deformed feet that splayed out like a frog's. But they seemed friendly, and they smiled and waved at Shanti.

The woman appeared, and in an ill-tempered way threw a banana leaf in front of each of them. She then proceeded to bring in trays of rice, vegetables and curried beans. Each boy grabbed handfuls of the food, put it on his leaf, and then stuffed it into his mouth. One boy with no hands used his toes as fingers. Shanti tried not to look, but the boy's agility was mesmerising. A sharp nudge from Ashiq reminded him to eat, and he bent his head and scooped food into his mouth, just like his new family.

The food was good, though Ashiq muttered that the amount of money uncle received from the beggars was enough to feed a hundred street children.

As they finished, the boys flung the used banana leaves into an old tin bin, and elbowed and jostled each other to get outside. Once outside, they unrolled their blankets and promptly lay down to sleep in their chosen place.

At least, Shanti thought, they were all going to sleep. As he settled down beside Ashiq, he was conscious of a movement towards them. The boys were pushing up to Ashiq and pleading in thin little voices,

"Tell us a story, Ashiq."

"Ashiq, please tell us a story."

"The one about the boat," implored a quavery voice.

"Ah! The boat!" smiled Ashiq.

"Yes, tell us about the boat," echoed the little voices.

Ashiq grinned at the questioning expression on Shanti's face and began,

"Once there were some poor boys with no family and they lived near a big river."

The boys smiled in satisfaction at the familiar story and snuggled down under their thin blankets.

"One day the rain poured down from the heavens. It rained for seven days and seven nights and the river became huge. Many trees from the riverside were uprooted. They floated down the big river and reached the place where the boys lived. There they jammed, all entangled in one another.

One seeing the trees the boys were filled with excitement. 'Let's make a big raft,' they shouted. 'Get some ropes.' So they set to, tied all the trees together and made a raft. Every boy helped, even those who had no hands. With much heaving and pulling, the poor boys launched it into the river and they all climbed onto it. 'We'll sail away,' they cried. 'We'll sail away and find a beautiful island.'

"The raft floated down the wide, wide river, and after a few days the boys spied an island. It was a beautiful island in the middle of the river. It had banana trees, green grass, beautiful birds and butterflies, and friendly animals." Ashiq paused for a moment and then asked, "And what do you think the boys did then?"

There was silence. No one replied. All the boys, snug under their blankets, had fallen asleep.

Ashiq smiled at an enthralled Shanti. "Every night they want a story and every night they all fall asleep."

"But I'm not asleep and I want to hear the ending, Ashiq."

Ashiq shook his head ruefully. "There is no ending, Shanti. It's a story without an ending, not even for you."

Ashiq lay down and stared for a long time at the millions of stars in the dark sky. Then he too fell asleep. In the night Shanti was disturbed by the furtive movements of several rats as they foraged around the rubbish in the yard.

Life for Shanti with Ashiq and the boys settled into a regular, if somewhat boring routine. Every day Shanti and Ashiq would trundle down to the bus station and perform. At dusk they would return to the shack, have their supper and then sleep. All their earnings were given to uncle and if any boy was found hiding his money he was thrown out of the compound. Uncle was very clever at guessing if money was being hidden and the woman, who had favourites, used them to spy and inform on the other boys.

However, Shanti adored Ashiq. Ashiq was like everyone's big brother. He cared for the smaller boys, listened to their grievances and cheered everyone up when the skies darkened and the dull heavy rain fell.

"One day we'll leave," Ashiq whispered to Shanti as he stared at the black clouds. "We'll build a boat and sail away."

"What about the boys?"

"Oh, they can come too, as long as they don't keep asking for stories." They both laughed, and Ashiq put his arm around Shanti and hugged him.

It was hot, so hot. Shanti's fingers slipped, holding the mallets. He had played all morning outside the bus station whilst Ashiq performed his acrobatics inside. At noon they sat together and nibbled on the pakoras that Ashiq had bought.

"I've not got many rupees, Ashiq."

"Never mind, I've collected enough."

Ashiq was sweating badly. His clothes stuck to him and his frizzy hair was plastered across his forehead. He pushed his pakoras away.

"Finish these, Shanti. I don't want any more."

"Are you feeling okay, Ashiq?"

"Yes! Yes! I'm just so hot." Ashiq wiped his face on his sleeve. "Well, back to work, Shanti boy. Must collect the rupees for uncle."

The boiling sun was disappearing into a haze of dust and fumes, when Shanti heard Ashiq calling him.

"Shanti! Shanti! Come here quickly!"

Shanti heaved his xylophone over his back and shuffled hurriedly into the bus station.

"Look!" exclaimed Ashiq, pointing excitedly. On the television, slung up high where waiting travellers could watch it, an athletics competition was taking place. They were not ordinary competitors.

"Look! Look, Shanti!"

The athletes had amputated or missing legs. The missing parts had been replaced by highly technical substitutes. Ashiq bounced up and down in excitement. One man had two steel supports shaped and cupped to his upper thighs. They ended in two highly stylised curves, which he balanced on. At a starting signal all the disabled athletes ran. Ran on their artificial legs and their speed was amazing.

"I want to run like that," Ashiq turned to Shanti, his eyes burning with excitement. "I want to run, Shanti."

"You shall! You shall, Ashiq." Shanti was convinced that Ashiq could achieve anything. "And you'll be the winner, Ashiq. The best runner of them all."

10

The Magic Man

That night Shanti asked Ashiq how he came to be living with uncle. Ashiq looked away and shook his head. Shanti thought he wasn't going to answer him, but then he turned back to Shanti.

"I had a terrible accident. A car driven by a drunken man ran into me. I was taken to hospital some distance away." Ashiq paused, frowning. "There was nothing they could do to save my legs." He bit his lip at the painful memory. "Anyway, I suppose it was easier for them to take them off. My family were very, very poor. They couldn't afford the fare to visit me and in the end I was left there. Nobody came to take me back home. I was seven, Shanti, seven."

"That's awful," whispered Shanti. "Who brought you here, Ashiq?"

"I think uncle used to visit the hospital to pick up sick abandoned boys. He would tell them he was a relative. He might have been, who knows? The hospital would let him take the boys away. I think they were glad to get rid of them. Anyway, that's how I arrived here, and that's enough talk about me, Shanti. I'm here, you're here." Ashiq smiled sadly. "And we are okay for the moment."

"Tell us a story, Ashiq."

The thin little voices had started their pleading.

"I don't feel like ..."

"Please, Ashiq! Please!"

This time, Ashiq, falteringly, told a different story.

"Once there was a man of magic. He could make things out of anything. Any piece of metal or plastic he would fashion into the most fantastic things." Ashiq stopped to wipe his sweating face. "One day some poor boys went to him. 'Please make me new feet out of that plastic,' said one, and so he did. 'Please make us new legs out of your special metal,' said others, and he did. 'I need some magic dust to stop me from shaking,' pleaded one boy, and the magic man obliged."

All the boys, at this point, were listening avidly and nodding in delight. Ashiq continued. "But there was this other boy who was different. He just wanted to stand. He had legs, but they were so twisted that he had no hope of being able to walk."

Shanti sat up on his blanket, all attention.

"Well, the magic man looked at him carefully. 'I can't help you,' he eventually said. 'You must go to the very best hospital in the city. They can do wonderful things and one day you will be able to stand.'"

Shanti frowned and looked very doubtful at this bit of the story. He pulled at Ashiq's sleeve.

"I want special magic legs too, Ashiq," he whispered.

"No, Shanti boy. Magic is for the no-hopers. One day you will have what is possible, and it will have nothing to do with magic."

Ashiq, exhausted, lay back and closed his eyes.

Next morning Shanti woke up and reached over to rouse Ashiq. He couldn't wake him. Ashiq's face was a strange grey colour. A film of sweat covered it, and his eyes stayed closed. Frantically Shanti shook him, then getting no response he scrambled over the beggar boys' sleeping bodies to uncle's door. He banged desperately on it.

"Uncle! Uncle! Come quickly. Ashiq's ill."

No response. Shanti banged even louder.

"Open up, uncle. Ashiq's ill."

The door opened and uncle's bad-tempered face scowled down at Shanti.

"Ill? Who's ill?"

"It's Ashiq, uncle. I can't wake him."

"He's probably being idle." Uncle turned around, impatient to get back into the shack.

"No, uncle! No! He looks ill. He really does."

Shanti was almost sobbing with frustration. What was the matter with this stupid man?

Seeing Shanti's distraught face, uncle hesitated, then waddled out onto the veranda. Pushing the now awake and anxious boys aside, he leaned over to look at Ashiq.

"Hm, he looks bad. Probably needs to sleep it off."

"No, uncle! Do something now! Get a rickshaw to take him to hospital," screamed Shanti. "He's very ill!"

Uncle glared at Shanti and was just about to yell at him when he thought better of it. He hurried outside to call a rickshaw.

"Don't leave me, Shanti," a faint cry came from Ashiq. "Don't leave me."

"I won't! I won't!" Shanti grabbed at Ashiq's arm.

Uncle came back and lifted Ashiq's limp body up. He made his way through the wailing boys, with Shanti scrabbling after him.

Ashiq was dumped into a rickshaw and the driver told to take him downtown to the nearest hospital. Shanti clung to the step of the rickshaw and hauled himself up.

"You're not going!" snarled uncle.

"I am going! Ashiq needs me."

"Well, keep your mouth shut!"

Uncle threw some rupees at the rickshaw driver and stamped off.

At the hospital the rickshaw driver lifted Ashiq's unconscious body down. Shanti hurried after him. The driver carried Ashiq inside and placed him on a bench. A doctor came over to them.

"What's this?" He looked with concern at Ashiq and bent over him to take his pulse.

"I don't know", replied the driver. "He was thrown into my rickshaw."

The doctor took the man aside and questioned him carefully. He wrote some things down in his notepad and made a phone call from his mobile, then returned to Ashiq. The driver departed. Shanti was desperately holding Ashiq's hand and speaking to him.

"Ashiq, Ashiq, you'll get better," faltered Shanti. "Then we'll save all our rupees and buy you those special metal legs. And you'll run, Ashiq, you'll be the best runner." Tears ran down his face.

The doctor looked kindly at Shanti. He hesitated, then said slowly,

"Let me take your friend. I'm very sorry, but he's said goodbye to this world."

"No!" whispered Shanti. "He can't have. He's going to be a famous runner. I was just telling him." Then, "Ashiq! Ashiq!"

Quickly signalling to a watching nurse, who wheeled a trolley over, the doctor gently unclasped Shanti's hand from that of Ashiq. He lifted Ashiq onto the trolley. Looking down at Shanti's tearful face, he said very seriously,

"I think that your friend died from a very infectious disease. I have informed the authorities. Please wait here. When I come back I'd like to do some tests on you, young man."

He then wheeled Ashiq quickly away.

Shanti stared dumbly after them.

"Go on your boat, Ashiq," he called after him. "Go to that wonderful island."

Then he remembered that the boat story had no ending. Did the raft ever stop? Had it stopped for Ashiq? With a sob, he scuttled out of the hospital.

The rickshaw man was still standing outside, talking to some other men. He looked with concern at Shanti's distraught face.

"How's your friend, then?"

"He's, he's..." Shanti couldn't continue.

The driver nodded understandingly.

"Do you want me to take you back?"

"Well, yes, I suppose so. I'll have to leave him." He stared back the hospital. "Thank you." Then, "Goodbye Ashiq."

It was all a nightmare to poor Shanti. He hauled himself into the rickshaw and was taken back to uncle's.

The gate was open, the yard deserted. Shanti looked round in bewilderment.

"Shanti," a voice hissed from the side of the veranda. It was the boy with the deformed feet. "There's been a police raid. Uncle's arrested and the boys have all been taken to the hospital. They said something about infection. They didn't see me. I hid from everyone, behind the bin."

"What are you going to do?" asked a bewildered Shanti.

"I'm off to the train station. You can earn money there and sleep on the station. Where's Ashiq?"

"Dead," whispered Shanti, scarcely able to utter the word. "Dead."

"Dead?" the boy looked shocked, then gazed fearfully around. "Well, I'm off! Don't let them catch you, Shanti. Take care." He hobbled off.

"My xylophone," remembered Shanti. "I must get my xylophone." Hurriedly shuffling over to the veranda, he saw it in the corner. Slinging it over his back, he was just about to leave when he spotted Ashiq's abandoned truck lying forlornly on its side. He righted it and, for a second, sadly laid his arms across it.

"You can take away that garbage!" A harsh voice came from the door of the shack. "I told him you would all bring us bad luck. Curses on the lot of you!" The woman stomped up to Shanti. "Everything is ruined because of that crippled Ashiq!, she ranted, waving her hands in the air. "And what am I to do now?"

Shanti felt a great anger rising furiously in him. He hissed at her, "Beg! You can beg like we do. Like Ashiq had to do! Earn your keep. Beg!"

"Get out!" she screamed at him. "Get out! You useless piece of crippled rubbish!"

Shanti grabbed Ashiq's truck, flung himself into it, and fled.

11

Hamid the Blind Boy

There were no familiar faces at the railway station. Perhaps that was not surprising. Hundreds of people were milling around, waiting for trains. Every so often the huge wooden doors to the platforms would burst open and great crowds of people would surge through. Then there would be a confused entanglement of suitcases, porters, families, workers and station officials, all swirling around in a whirlpool of frantic activity. People looked in a state of anxiety.

Where was grandad, aunty, little Rafi, the cases, the taxi, the exit?

Slowly the confusing mix-up sorted itself out. The station waiting area would calm down for a few minutes until the next train departed or arrived.

Shanti sat in Ashiq's truck and peered into the station. He realised that he was feeling hungry, having had no food since the previous night. What's more, he had no money and that was serious. Back to work, Shanti boy, he said to himself, and hurriedly repressed the feeling of overwhelming sadness at the thought of Ashiq.

He slowly pushed himself, in the cart, along the pavement at the side of the station until he came to a crossroads. Beyond the crossroads he could see a quiet square. I'll play there, he thought. Not many people about, but I need some peace.

Propelling his cart under a large shady tree, Shanti then climbed out and placed his xylophone on the ground. A slight breeze ruffled the leaves. Shanti looked up, listened intently, and then, smiling sadly to himself, proceeded to play. He played for his grandmother, for baba and for his special friend Ashiq. For a moment he forgot his lonely self and lost himself in his music. He played for a very long time.

That evening he returned to the station, pushed the truck under a bench and wriggled underneath beside it.

The man sleeping on the bench was unaware of the young boy hidden beneath.

Next day, he once again propelled himself down to the little square. The air felt hot and humid. Heavy rumblings tore through the darkening clouds, but no rain had yet appeared.

On reaching the square he abruptly stopped. Someone was standing near his tree. Shanti stared in disbelief. A tall thin boy of about twelve with a long sad face was holding something. A tin begging bowl was on the ground at his feet. Shanti felt annoyed: it was his pitch and the boy had stolen it. He started to yell, but stopped when the boy started to play.

The boy's fingers fluttered over and stroked his wooden instrument. He pursed his lips and blew. Softly the music he made floated over the square. It floated and soared into the branches of the tall tree and was carried away by the wind which heralded the rain. Indeed, fat raindrops began pouring from the sky and Shanti trundled quickly over to the tree for shelter. He stopped near the boy and gazed at him. The boy hadn't noticed him: was he blind?

"Hey! You make great music."

Quickly the boy turned his head and looked sightlessly in the direction of Shanti.

"Do you want my money? Have it! Take it! You always do! I wish I was dead!"

A shocked Shanti sat back in his truck.

"I don't want your money and what did you say? Dead? Nobody should wish they were dead."

"Well, I do!" The boy flung himself on the ground and silently wept. His thin shoulders heaved up and down.

Shanti pulled himself closer and awkwardly patted the boy's back. The boy shook his hand away.

"What's your name?"

"Hamid," he whispered, "and I'm blind."

"Well, Hamid, my name is Shanti and I'm crippled. I can't walk. I trundle everywhere in Ashiq's..." he stopped himself quickly. "No, not Ashiq's... in my truck." He bit his lip and shoved away his memories.

Gropingly, Hamid's hand reached out and felt the sides of Shanti's truck.

"Now, what's making you so unhappy, Hamid?" asked a now intrigued Shanti.

"The bad boys steal my rupees and the man who looks after me beats me if I don't earn enough money. I don't think I've earned much yet."

"No, you haven't," said Shanti, peering into Hamid's near-empty begging bowl.

Hamid worriedly pulled a face. The rain was beginning to bounce off the ground and Shanti was getting wet.

"Let's move closer to the tree trunk, Hamid. We'll sit down and talk, because I think I've got a plan."

He pushed his truck up to the tree and clambered out. Hamid stood up, listened, followed him and sat down next to him.

"Now, my name's Shanti and I play the xylophone. Now why don't you and I join up?"

"Join up?" Hamid looked puzzled. "Do you make music, Shanti?"

"Yes! We could play together, you and I, Hamid. Share the money."

"Well, I'm not so sure. I'm blind. I need someone to help me, show me ..."

"Yes! Yes!" Shanti impatiently interrupted him. "I can help you."

"Yes, but what about Uncle and those others who steal my money?"

"We can dodge them, Hamid. Come on, what do you say? We could be a good team."

There was a pause, Hamid's sensitive face frowned and then suddenly smiled.

"Things couldn't get worse, could they, Shanti?"

"You've decided, then?"

Hamid nodded vigorously. "Yes, I'll come with you, Shanti, and we'll be a team." Hamid clutched at Shanti's arm and squeezed it tight.

"Play me something, Shanti. I want to hear your music."

Shanti lifted the xylophone from out of the truck. He gently tapped the wooden slats on his instrument, making sharp staccato sounds just like the rain. He then speeded up his playing and the raindrops exploded into a sparkling shower. Hamid lifted his flute to his lips and the boys joined together in an intricate melody of rain, wind, clouds and the shining sun. They finished their playing as the rain stopped. Shanti clasped Hamid's hand.

"Wonderful," breathed Hamid. "We are brothers in our music and, Shanti, we will be brothers in our lives."

12

Making Music

So Shanti and Hamid became partners and the best of friends.

Shanti pushed a piece of string through a hole in the wood at the back of his truck and tied it. Hamid was then able to hang on to the loose end and follow Shanti.

After playing at various places around the city they would make their way back to the railway station. They bought pakoras from a food vendor and then hid themselves away behind some rubbish bins. Sleep was difficult: they were squashed against a wall and the bins smelled. The station was very noisy. No matter the time there was a constant movement of people and loud announcements of imminent arrivals and departures. One night the station police appeared and threw the homeless people out of the station. They failed to spot Shanti and Hamid, who, hearing the shouts and whistles, squeezed themselves even further behind the bins.

The day after the police raid Hamid and Shanti felt exhausted. They carefully crawled out from behind the bins and sat down beside a bench. An elderly lady, sitting on the bench, looked down at them, then muttered something to a young girl sitting next to her. The girl quickly got up, went to a food stall and came back with four large samosas. She bent down and handed them to Shanti.

"Have these," she smiled.

Shanti looked at the delicate hand holding the package. The girl had painted her nails a pale pink colour, and several pretty rings encircled her fingers. He was suddenly very aware of his grubby hands and quickly snatched at the food.

"Thank you. Thank you," he muttered in embarrassment.

The girl smiled down at him, which confused him even more. He stuffed the samosas beside him, and turned to Hamid.

"Let's go, Hamid."

Hamid scrambled to his feet and, holding onto the string, followed Shanti outside. They stayed by the station doors munching on the samosas.

"Let's stay here today, Shanti. I feel too tired to walk far." Hamid felt in Shanti's truck for his bowl and placed it in front of him.

"Okay," agreed Shanti. "We'll play here today."

He climbed out of the truck and lifted out his xylophone. They started with a lively jig, the flute and xylophone intertwining. Hamid slowed down and played a delicate little dance by himself. Shanti joined in, played faster and created a wild, skipping tune. Hamid then stopped, put his flute in his pocket and clapped his hands in time to the beat.

Many people stopped to throw coins until the music was interrupted by three unpleasant-looking youths.

"So you've got yourself a crippled mate? Double protection money you owe us now."

They stood in front of Hamid, snarling in his frightened face.

Before Shanti could react, they picked up Hamid's bowl and emptied it. Then: "Suckers! See you!" Smirking, they ran off into the crowd.

Hamid was shocked. His hand reached down to clutch at Shanti's shoulder. "Those are the boys, Shanti. I recognise their voices. They've always stolen my money. I tried to hide it, but they always found it. What can we do about it?" His voice shook.

Shanti was furious. How dare they just walk up and rob them?

"I'll have to think, Hamid. There must be some way of stopping them. I'll think of something; don't upset yourself. This is a good spot and we're not moving," he said with a confidence he was far from feeling.

Next day, Shanti thought he spotted them coming into the station. He yanked Hamid along and they hid themselves down an alley and in the doorway of a disused warehouse. After holding their breath and Shanti peeping round the corner, they decided to play somewhere else. It was the easiest way to avoid the gang.

Cautiously, ever alert, they trundled off to a large shopping centre, dodging in and out of the crowds and earning curses and kicks at the truck.

The shops and stores were selling everything one could ever need. Vegetables, flowers, pots, pans, spices, televisions, stoves, computers, phones, gold, silver, saris, books, magazines, sportswear and city suits. The variety went on and on.

Shanti looked up at a huge glass shop window. The plastic models, clad in their pretty saris, seemed to be waving and smiling at him. He gave a grin to himself: get real, Shanti boy, they are too beautiful to be looking at you.

He caught sight of his reflection in the window and suddenly felt depressed. Releasing his grip on the wheels, he waved madly at himself and pulled a horrible face. He squinted his eyes, stuck his tongue out, waggled it and jerked his head from side to side. Feeling much better, he continued on.

He decided to stop by a large department store. The store was on a corner site and its double doors opened onto the junction of two streets. The doors banged backwards and forwards as the people pushed to go in and out. Shanti thought it an okay place because people coming out either hesitated before crossing the road, or stopped and thought about which road to take. The emerging shoppers might also have some change in their pockets.

Shanti positioned himself and Hamid by the door, but on the side that led to the quieter of the streets. This meant that their music could be heard and they weren't in the way of anybody.

They were now becoming a very good duo. Shanti instinctively knew when to accompany the flute's melody and when to assert the rhythmic strengths of the xylophone. Hamid's flute solos were magic. Shanti often closed his eyes immersing himself in Hamid's playing. He was always woken abruptly by Hamid bending down and playing the flute loudly in his ear.

"No need for that, Hamid," he would say. "I'm listening to every note."

"Yes, but how long do you expect me to accompany your dreamings?"

Shanti would grin to himself and bang the mallets up and down the xylophone until Hamid begged him to stop.

It was fun. The boys earned money and some people actually stopped to listen. This pleased Shanti. He loved having an audience. Once a large dog sat with them howling at the sounds. People laughed and threw more coins. They used the same site for several weeks. At first the doorman disliked them. He guarded the door and kept the riff-raff out. Scruffy youths were held by the arms, whirled through the doors and pitched out onto the street. They then slouched off, hunching their shoulders in embarrassment. Nobody challenged the doorman; he was far too imposing. He was a huge man with a dark blue turban and a fierce, pointy, black moustache. He welcomed respectable people into the store and carried their bags out through the doors. Hamid and Shanti were scowled at and told to move away. They shuffled sideways for a few yards but continued playing. When he went inside they quietly shuffled back. He then ignored them. After a few days Shanti saw him leaning on the store wall, chewing on a piece of naan and tapping his foot to their music. He caught Shanti staring at him, his moustache twitched and he actually smiled. After that he sometimes brought them pakoras or fresh mango juice.

"Great, kids," he would say. "Great music," and he'd give a little skip as he pushed back through the doors.

Shanti and Hamid relaxed; they seemed to have avoided their tormentors.

13

The Robbery

E venings were good downtown. The sun had gone below
the skyline. It was cooler, lights had been switched on
and people were happily shopping or eating at the
many cafes and restaurants along the main street. Across
the street, diagonally from where they played, was a large
jewellery shop. A dazzling display of gold necklaces, bracelets,
rings and ornaments filled the window. Many wealthy people
alighted from chauffeur-driven cars and glided into the shop.
Shanti glimpsed the assistants lifting trays of sparking jewels
out of the window to show their customers. He laughed to
himself as he wondered if he would ever buy a gold ring, but
then quickly decided that there were hundreds of things he
would like before a ring. A new truck, for instance. Ashiq's
contraption, for he still thought of it as Ashiq's, needed a
new wheel. The front one was decidedly wonky. Shanti put
down his xylophone to examine it. Yes, the spokes were loose
and bent. He leaned even further forward to look at the axle.
Perhaps it, too, needed straightening.

Hamid had finished his solo and was taking a little rest.
He needed some time out to think about how he could
develop the winsome tune he'd composed. He took a rag
out of his pocket and began polishing his flute, his gentle
face frowning with an inward concentration.

Two men came to stand by the side of the boys. They were oblivious to them, or they just didn't rate them as being important. One man spoke into a mobile phone. It was their furtive manner and whispering that alerted Shanti. He kept his head down and squinted sideways at them. He held his breath. Hamid continued his inward composing and the polishing of his flute. The men then pulled their scarves up over their mouths and ran at a trot across to the jewellery shop. Without thinking, Shanti leapt along the pavement, burst through the department shop doors and grabbed at the trousers of the doorman.

"Robbery!" he yelled up at him. "The jeweller's shop is being robbed!"

The door man gaped at Shanti, then, suddenly understanding, dashed through the big doors. Shanti followed.

Across the road all was quiet. Then, mayhem!!

There was a loud bang from inside the jewellery shop. Next, a pick-up truck screeched along the street, pulling up with squealing tyres. Two other men leapt off the back of the truck. They ran at the window with a long metal pole. The window shattered, alarm bells were set off and the men grabbed at the gold in the smashed windows. The door of the shop flew open and customers fell out onto the street. Several of them lay still, their heads bleeding. After them leapt the two men who had stood near Shanti. They were waving revolvers and scaring back the crowds. The doorman stopped running towards the shop when the gunmen appeared, and turned around quickly. Shanti's truck lay on the pavement in front of him. He ran towards it, picked it up and hurled it. It went spinning through the air, making an arc like a giant Frisbee, and skidded along the ground in front of the running men.

They stumbled over it, lost their balance and fell headlong. The doorman sprinted towards them, knocked their guns out of their hands, walloped one in the eye, and with a heavy fist smashed one on the nose. They both rolled on the tarmac, moaning in pain and spilling the stolen jewellery.

Meanwhile the pick-up had raced off, only to be stopped by several siren-wailing police cars. The men were forced out, handcuffed and thrown into a police wagon. Several policemen then ran down to where the doorman was sitting on the two accomplices.

Shanti was bouncing up and down with excitement. The doorman was his hero, and it was his truck that had stopped the thieves.

Abruptly his excitement drained from him. The man - or was he a teenager - that the police were handcuffing, looked familiar. Shanti pushed himself through the crowds to get a better view. He wriggled to the front and saw Rajiv; yes, it was Rajiv. He was handcuffed and being taken away by the police. Shanti remembered the puppeteer's words: 'And he will do it again'. He shrank back into the crowd. There was no helping Rajiv now.

All this time Hamid had been practising his new tune. He had winced at the bangs and screeches, but had serenely played on. Shanti sat and looked at him. He missed so much of life, being blind. But then again, thought Shanti, he had an inner life all of his own and to him it was as exciting and fulfilling as that of many sighted people. He looked round to find his xylophone. It had been pushed against the wall and the mallets were in the gutter. He picked them up. The sound of ambulances, police cars and loud voices faded away as Hamid asked reproachfully,

"What was all that about, Shanti? I couldn't hear myself playing."

"It was nothing Hamid, nothing."

Shanti paused, then added,

"Just the end of a sad story."

The doorman was rewarded for his bravery by being appointed head of security for several department stores.

Before he left his doorman's job, he took Shanti and Hamid to an ice-cream parlour and treated them to two enormous ice-creams. The owner of the parlour frowned when he saw the two scruffy boys and the battered truck. But a stern look from the doorman made him eager to help. He lifted Shanti onto a chair, tucked the truck by the wall, guided Hamid to his place and went off to get the two large ice-creams the doorman had ordered.

It looked like a procession. First the owner came in, carrying a large ice-cream with lit sparklers shooting little flames into the air. Behind him came a waitress carrying another ice-cream covered in hot chocolate, with cherries perched on the top. Lastly came a kitchen boy holding a large bottle of Kingfisher beer. It was a free gift: the doorman's fame had spread. There were whisperings and noddings in the ice-cream parlour, then a sudden eruption of clapping and shouts of

"Bravo!" and

"Well done!"

The doorman stood up and waved his clenched hands above his head. The ice-creams were placed in front of the boys. The waitress pulled out the sparklers for Shanti to wave around excitedly, until they went out and she took them away. He then stared down at the pile of white stuff in his dish.

The doorman laughed, put a spoon in Hamid's hand, scooped up some ice-cream, hot chocolate and a cherry, and guided it towards Hamid's mouth.

"Open!" he commanded. "Now, what do you think of that?"

"It's too cold and hot," Hamid yelped in alarm, hanging his tongue out. But then he chewed on the cherry, swallowed it and opened his mouth for another spoonful. The doorman laughed and guided his hand to spoon up some more. Hamid quickly got the hang of it.

The boys had never tasted ice-cream before. Shanti, frowning, pushed his around with his spoon until a fierce look from the doorman forced him to try some. He held it in his mouth with an astonished look on his face. Then he swallowed it.

"Mm," grinned Shanti, "It's yummy. I think I like ice-cream."

"Mm", agreed Hamid. "Yummy, yummy, I know I like ice-cream."

Then there was quiet as the boys quickly scooped up the yummy stuff. On noses, chins, cheeks and the table, the ice-cream was accidentally smeared everywhere. The doorman sipped his beer and smiled indulgently at them. Round the dish scraped Shanti's spoon, picking up the last of the delicious treat. He then held Hamid's hand for him whilst he scooped up all the bits he had missed. The one remaining cherry Hamid insisted on giving to Shanti.

14

Attack

The boys were outside the railway station in the mid-morning heat. The fumes from the traffic made the sultry air thick and uncomfortable to breathe.

Shanti and Hamid had given up on the department store. The one time they had returned, after their friend had left, they were driven away by a new, nasty doorman.

"Riff-raff! Clear off!" he'd yelled at them, kicking the truck and knocking over their begging bowl. So they had scarpered.

Shanti was sitting on the pavement, peering at his truck's axle. People raced around them, hurrying to catch trains or leap into taxis.

"It's all bent, Hamid," he moaned, "And I can't straighten it."

"Oh dear!" murmured Hamid, his thoughts elsewhere.

"Are you listening, Hamid?" Shanti continued dramatically. "My truck needs some help. It's got a poor bent axle. It's a hero! It flew through the air and stopped the bad men. Wham! Slam! Gotcha!"

He pretended to cry.

"Boo-hoo! My axle is all bent and hurting. Hamid will have to carry me, a poorly brave truck, on his strong, strong back."

Hamid laughed out loud.

"You need some help for your poor, bent head and your poor, bent legs!"

"Okay! Okay! I know I'm a bit crazy, but the axle does need to be straightened, Hamid, and I can't do it."

"Well, take it to a garage."

"Oh, yes! And say: 'Can you fix my Harley Davidson please?'" Shanti thought for a moment. "Well, I suppose I could try, but what about paying them?"

"Take the money in the bowl."

"Are you sure?"

"'Course I am. It's a necessity for the poor brave truck."

"All right! All right! Now, you wait here, Hamid, and don't move till I come back. I won't be very long."

Shanti remembered seeing a garage around the back of the station. He pushed his truck to the end of the front wall, turned down a side street, avoided all the broken paving and heaps of smouldering rubbish, and reached the back road.

Across the road was the garage. Men were sitting and standing, wielding hammers and power drills, which they drove into obsolete car engines, dismembering them and retrieving usable bits. Others were welding unrecognisable lumps of metal onto something else. One car was held aloft by ropes attached to four wooden poles. A man seemed to be attacking its underside with a huge spanner. Old tyres, wheels, hubs, seats, doors and steering wheels littered the pavement, and there was a raucous noise of Indian pop music blaring over the street. Shanti hesitated before attempting to negotiate his truck down from the pavement to cross over.

He noticed them first and his eyes widened in fear. They were sauntering along on the far pavement, smoking *bidis*, hands in pockets and eyes darting about, looking for easy pickings. Glancing across the road, they saw him. Shanti gave a sharp intake of breath, grasped his wheels, pushed off and hurtled along the pavement. The youths gave a delighted whoop, flicked away their cigarettes and chased after him.

At the end of the street the sad figure of a young girl paused in her walk and leaned against the station wall. Shanti frantically turned the wheels and hurtled along the pavement. He couldn't get away. He'd never escape them. Shanti's heart thumped louder and louder as he pushed with all his strength at the wonky wheels.

Down the pavement he hurtled, almost plunging off the edge. Then, horror! His truck tipped up as one of the youths leapt onto the back. Shanti was thrown out, cracking his head hard on the pavement.

"Pay up! Pay up!" they snarled. The gang were on him. He felt his shirt being yanked apart, and long clawing fingers pulling the rupees out of his pocket.

"Get off! Get off!" Another high voice joined in the shouting. He was aware of the prying fingers leaving him. On looking up, through his matted hair and seeping blood, he saw that a girl had leapt on the back of the biggest youth and was yanking at his hair.

"Get off! Get off!"

Wham! A body hit the pavement near him. He received a kick in the ribs from another youth, and then they ran off.

People had appeared, alerted by the commotion. They saw that the two children weren't dead, so they lost interest and moved away.

Shanti moaned out loud. His head hurt. He could feel blood trickling down his face. His side was an agony of pain. He must get away. Where was his truck? Through his matted strands of hair he saw it, lying on its side, further down the pavement. Gasping with pain, he crossed his legs over each other and attempted to crawl to his truck.

"Stop! Where are you going?" A gentle, anxious voice reached him. He turned to look at the girl who had come to his help. She had pushed herself up on her elbows and her face was frowning at him in concern. Her long dark plait had come undone in her wrestling with one of the gang. Her hair flowed across her face and over her shoulders. Light brown eyes regarded him questioningly, and when she smiled encouragingly at him he noticed a small gap between her very white front teeth. Shanti wanted to get away. He didn't know how to respond to gentle concern.

"What's it to you?" he muttered at her.

"You're hurt. Your head is bleeding."

He turned his head, not wanting to speak to her.

She questioned him some more.

Please shut up, he thought. But then she said,

"Why don't you come back with me and I'll clean you up?"

"No! I don't want to!"

"Come on," she said kindly, "What's your name?"

"Shanti!" he blurted out, "It's Shanti."

"Well, mine's Rupa and I have a little sister called Amrita and," she laughed, "we have a dog named Danva and a home by the big church."

15

Family

The girl painfully stood up. She rubbed at her side, then limped over to retrieve his truck. She grasped him under his arms and lifted him in. How light he was, like an injured bird.

Shanti grimaced in agony and a wave of sickness engulfed him. He offered no resistance as the girl bent over and began pushing his truck. He heard her little gasps of pain as she shoved the truck over the uneven pavement.

Feebly, Shanti attempted to help, but a wave of dizziness overwhelmed him and his head slumped down onto his chest. He was aware of the truck bumping up and down, and then a sudden lurch as the truck stopped. The girl seemed to be forcing one of the front wheels back on. Another lurch, as this time the truck careered sideways and almost tipped him out. Shanti held onto the sides and waited for the earth to stop whirling. He heard the girl's breathing become increasingly laboured as she struggled to keep the truck moving. He forced himself to sit upright and push at the wheels.

They eventually turned into a narrow, garbage-littered alley, which opened onto a lane, bordering a large black church. Tall iron railings surrounded the church, and tied to them were planks and tarpaulin sheets. People were living in these makeshift dwellings. Shanti was eyed curiously, but then the slum dwellers turned to continue their various activities. The girl pushed him towards the end tent.

Outside the tent, looking anxiously down the lane, was a small girl of about seven. She was wearing a long tunic that looked several sizes too big. Round her middle was a cord. She'd pulled the bottom half of the tunic up and over the cord to lift it off the ground. The small girl jumped about and waved excitedly when she saw them, but was puzzled when she noticed Shanti.

"Who have your brought home, Rupa?"

"This is Shanti, Amrita. He was being set upon by some nasty lads. He hurt his head, so I brought him back with me."

Rupa, turned towards the tent, spoke some more words to Amrita and then disappeared inside. She emerged carrying a metal bucket and strode purposefully off.

Amrita looked down at Shanti. Long black eyelashes framed her lively light brown eyes. Dimples appeared in her round cheeks as she smiled kindly at him. Shanti was filled with embarrassment. He frowned at her and attempted to ignore her. If his head hadn't hurt so much he would have scuttled off. Amrita continued looking at him. Loose black curls touched the sides of her pretty face and her voice was full of concern as she spoke to him.

"You poor boy," she said in a motherly way.

Shanti cringed and frowned once again at her. Amrita wasn't in the least put off by Shanti's scowling looks.

"What happened to your poor little legs and who looks after you?"

I don't have to answer this, though Shanti crossly. Nosey kid, wanting to know everything.

Undeterred by his sulky silence, Amrita continued smiling down at him.

"My legs were always like this," Shanti suddenly blurted out. "I was born with them and nobody looks after me. I'm ten and I look after myself." Now shut up, he thought, I can't stand any more questions.

Amrita quietly nodded, sat down beside him and stroked his arm and his matted hair.

An irritated Shanti almost slapped her hand away. But then she crooned to him,

"I'm seven, Rupa is fourteen and she looks after me. Our mother is dead. Look at your clothes, Shanti, all ragged and dirty, we could look after you."

She continued to stroke his hair and pat his arm.

"Stay with us, Shanti. Stay with Rupa and me and we'll look after you."

Shanti suddenly felt dizzy again. He closed his eyes and swayed towards Amrita. He felt her soft curls on his face and her warm little hand stroking him. His poor aching head drooped onto her shoulder. He gave up all resistance and leaned on Amrita.

'One day we'll build a boat and sail away.' Ashiq's words swam into his mind. Now he, Shanti, was sailing away. He was escaping, he was going down that big river in a boat but Amrita, not Ashiq, was with him.

"Stay with us, Shanti," whispered the gentle voice. "Stay with Rupa and me. We'll look after you."

Shanti slept, but was dragged back to reality by Rupa appearing with the bucket and some soap.

He was propelled into the tent, lifted out of the truck and his tattered shirt pulled carefully off. He closed his eyes tightly as cold water and soap was sponged over his head and down his body.

Rupa patted him dry with the inside of his shirt and he felt a new top being pulled over his head. His unresisting arms were slid into the sleeves.

He wanted to resist. He wanted to assert himself and tell them to lay off. He didn't want to be spoken to softly and kindly; he wasn't used to it. But then he'd tried for so long. He'd tried to help his grandmother, Rajiv and Ashiq. All had ended in disaster. Perhaps it was time to give up for a little while and let someone else care for him?

He opened his eyes and looked at the sympathetic faces of the two girls. Looking down, he saw that he was now wearing a clean, blue, cotton top. Tentatively he stroked it with the tips of his fingers. It was the same colour as a soft shawl his grandmother had once worn. Without knowing why, he felt tears flow into his eyes and then spill down his cheeks. Trying to stop them, he choked on a sob. He felt the girls' arms encircle him and hug him.

"You can stay with us," he heard Rupa say. "You can, Shanti, that is if you would like to?"

Shanti gave a big gulp and tried to nod and to smile. Then a picture of Hamid waiting for him at the station flashed into his mind. Hamid, all alone and helpless. Shanti screwed his fists into his eyes and sobbed out loud.

"I can't stay," he blurted out. "I have a friend who's blind. He's waiting for me and he won't move till I go and get him."

Rupa clutched at her hair. One boy she could just about cope with, but two? One was crippled and one couldn't see. How could they manage? But they both needed help and they had no one. They were even worse off than Amrita and herself.

"What's his name?" she asked in a sudden rush. "I'll go and fetch him. Where is he? You two stay here and wait for me."

Amrita grabbed her sister's hand and kissed it.

16

Life is Good

There was an awkward silence in the tent when Rupa left. Shanti was embarrassed to have cried in front of Amrita. He rubbed nervously at his knuckles. Amrita avoided looking at him and twiddled her curls with one of her fingers. How long they might have sat like this is difficult to guess, but the silence was at last broken by a snuffling noise. A long hairy nose pushed up through the flap of the tent.

"Danva!!" shrieked Amrita. She leapt up and hugged a big mangy dog that had managed to wriggle into the tent and was now panting in delight at Amrita's attentions. "Look, Shanti, this is our dog."

"My dog?"

"Yes, yours and Hamid's and mine and Rupa's."

"I'm not sure I like dogs."

"That's because you don't know him. He's very, very special; he looks after himself."

"Well, what's he doing here then?" snapped Shanti.

Amrita ignored his sarcasm.

"Now he's looking after us," she giggled to herself. "But it won't be for long: he goes off to visit other friends."

"Oh, does he? He told you that, did he?"

Amrita frowned at Shanti, opened her eyes very wide and patiently said,

"Shanti, he's a dog. He doesn't talk. I can just guess what he's up to."

Amrita tickled Danva's ear. He licked her hand and rolled onto his back, waving his paws in the air.

"Ugh! He's got red patches all over him."

"Only a few," retorted Amrita, stroking his fur. "Poor, poor Danva with lots of red patches."

Shanti felt a surge of jealousy at the loving attention Danva was receiving. He remembered how Amrita had crooned to him. Giving Danva a petulant scowl, he hurriedly scuttled outside to his truck. Amrita jumped up and followed him.

"Where are you going? You're not leaving?" she asked anxiously.

"No, I'm not leaving," muttered Shanti. "I just want to show you something."

He lifted his xylophone out of his truck and scrutinised it. Wiping the dust off with his fingers, he saw with relief that it was all in one piece and none of the wooden slats had shaken loose. Baba had constructed it carefully and strongly.

Amrita squatted beside him and Shanti grinned at her curious expression. He tucked the xylophone under his arm, shuffled into the tent and placed it on the floor. Danva sniffed at it suspiciously.

"What is it?" frowned Amrita, touching one of the slats.

"Guess."

"I can't."

"Go on, have a try."

Amrita sat down and stared fixedly at the xylophone. She chewed her lips in concentration.

"Is it a little bed for a baby?"

"No."

"Is it a little table for me?"

"No."

"Is it a little gate for a garden?"

"No." Shanti smiled at the memory of his first guess.

"Is it a little..? Oh, I give up, Shanti. I'll never guess. Just tell me."

Shanti carefully removed the mallets. Danva gave a low growl, backed towards the tent flap and slipped outside.

"Close your eyes, Amrita," Shanti commanded. "Don't peep. Close them tightly and listen."

Amrita did as she was told.

Shanti smiled at Amrita's serious little face with its tightly closed eyes.

Looking down at the xylophone, Shanti rippled his mallets along the slats. He made the sound of soap bubbles floating through the air. Amrita gave a little start, but didn't open her eyes. Slowly she pushed herself up onto her knees. Holding her arms out, she swayed gently in time to the music.

Takshaka, thought Shanti. Amrita is dancing for you.

But then he deliberately broke the spell by banging hard on the slats. Amrita opened her eyes and laughed at him. She jumped to her feet and spun round and round.

"What a surprise, Shanti! What a wonderful surprise!"

She sank to the floor as the music quietened, then up onto her tiptoes she leapt, whirling round the tent. Nimbly she danced around Shanti. Her black curls shook around her little head and her small brown toes pointed in one direction, then the other.

Barking and howling accompanied her wild leaping. Danva had nosed his way back into the tent and wanting to be part of the merriment.

"Out, dog!!!!"

The music ceased abruptly. Amrita stopped her cavorting, as she watched her sister guide a tall, thin, delicate-looking boy into the tent. The boy's eyes gazed sightlessly around.

"Hamid!" shouted Shanti in delight, "You've found us!"

That night, snuggled under a blanket behind a curtain that Rupa had tied up, Shanti whispered to Hamid.

"We've got a home now, Hamid."

Hamid nodded seriously.

"We can earn money, Hamid, and take care of Rupa and Amrita."

"We can," agreed Hamid. "We'll work very hard and bring them lots of rupees."

Our home! A home with Rupa and Amrita. Shanti grinned to himself.

"We've got a big sister and a little sister, Hamid."

"All thanks to Allah!" replied Hamid, and closed his eyes.

All thanks to me, Shanti thought. He heard Rupa moving about on the other side of the curtain. He felt her comforting presence. Closing his eyes, he too slept. Things were going to be all right.

By Maureen Roberts